2018

AWAKENING

COVENANT COLLEGE BOOK ONE

AMANDA M. LEE

WINCHESTERSHAW PUBLICATIONS

To Sydnee, who taught me how to live with others

1 ONE

"Why is everyone naked?"

It took me a second to register the comment. It took me another second to register the comment was from my father. It took me almost a full minute to respond.

"No one is naked. They're just not wearing shirts."

I was hoping he wouldn't make a big deal about this. I didn't want to be embarrassed before I even met these people.

I could hear my dad mutter something under his breath while my mom put a hand on his arm to soothe him. I hoped that would be enough prompting. If I had to pull out the fake tears, we were all going to be upset.

I was following my parents down the fifth floor corridor of Wharton Hall – my college dorm. As an incoming freshman, this was a nerve-wracking, and exciting day for me.

It had taken a lot of effort to talk my parents into letting me stay in a co-ed dorm. If Dad had his way, he would've forced me into an all-girls dorm – and that would have been ugly.

Actually, my mom didn't seem to care about the coed dorm. In fact, she's the one who ultimately changed Dad's mind.

"It will be safer for her to have boys around," she'd argued. "They can walk with the girls to their night classes and even go to parties with them."

Parties were another story, of course. Dad wanted to pretend those didn't exist. I found that pretty funny – especially since he was reportedly banned from all the bars in our small town when he was my age because he liked to fight a little too much – and fighting for him involved throwing furniture and people through windows.

My name is Zoe Lake. I'm eighteen years old, and I'm from a very small town in Northern Lower Michigan. It has one stoplight and six bars. Yeah, you do the math.

The town was so small I graduated with fifty-two people – one of whom was my own cousin. There weren't a lot of choices in classes, after-school activities or friends. I essentially made a choice in middle school: I was going to be popular. To achieve that goal, I aligned myself with the 'in crowd' for the duration of my stay in the district.

I didn't hate my friends, I just didn't particularly like them. I was just biding my time.

When it came time to select a college, I had a big decision to make. My grades were good enough to get me into one of the big state universities. Ultimately, though, two of my high school friends opted to go there – and I really didn't want to go to the same school they were attending for fear I'd fall into old patterns.

I wanted to go to a school where I didn't know anyone, hence Covenant College.

Covenant College is a mid-sized school in mid-Michigan. It's ninety minutes away from home – too far for my parents to stop in on a whim, but close enough I can go home on weekends. Looking around at all the shirtless beefcake preening in the hall – I doubted I would want to be too close to home on weekends.

My parents stopped outside room 506 and then turned to me expectantly.

I was a little nervous, but I didn't want them to think I was jittery in case they tried to help me make friends – like when I was in kindergarten. Instead, I took a deep breath to calm my frazzled nerves, tucked my shoulder-length blonde hair behind my ears, and opened the door.

Two girls in the common room greeted me. They were surrounded by their own belongings – which they hadn't yet moved into the adjoining bedroom.

I took a quick glance into the bedroom, noticing no one had laid claim to a bed. Since we were freshman, we only had the two rooms and one bathroom to share. The older we got, the better the dorm-room options.

I plastered a smile on my face. Even though I was an only child, I was determined to make this work. I'd heard my parents talking when they thought I couldn't hear them the other day. They didn't think I was capable of getting along with others. I'd show them – or at least I'd fake it until they left.

"I'm Zoe," I said, maneuvering around my parents.

I got a good look at the two girls. One was short and blonde like me. I'm about five feet, five inches tall and thin, without being waif-like. The first girl I focused on looked to be about five feet, three inches tall with shoulder-length blonde hair. She was a little chubbier than me, but not fat, and she had bright blue eyes. She was completely average looking. She smiled in greeting.

"I'm Brittany Hartman."

We were college students, so we didn't shake hands. Instead, we just exchanged tepid smiles. I could tell everyone was sizing each other up.

"This is Paris," Brittany said, nervously gesturing to the other girl.

This girl was a lot more interesting to look at. Paris was about five feet, seven inches tall with long, brown hair, and the highest cheek-bones I had ever seen on a real person (versus the pages of Vogue). She was also ridiculously pale and exotic looking.

"Hi."

"Hi," she said, smiling back.

My parents pulled my luggage into the middle of the room and watched me expectantly.

"What?"

"Do you want me to help you unpack?" Mom looked hopeful.

"I'm fine."

"No, you should get unpacked right away."

"I'm fine." I didn't need my mommy to help me put my clothes away. Plus, I would die if my dad saw the lingerie in my bag. He still thought I was a virgin – even though he'd found my birth control pills a few months ago and asked my mom if they were drugs.

The subject hadn't been brought up again. I had a feeling, if he saw what was in my bag, he'd blow.

"She's fine," Dad warned. "They can all unpack together."

Mom looked uncertain. I could tell she didn't want to leave me. *Ah, the burden of being an only child.*

"We should just get her settled ... ." Mom bit her lower lip.

Dad was warily eyeing the shirtless boys in the hall who were showing an overt interest in Paris and me as they copped an occasional glance. "No, we're going. I want to get home in time to get some yard work done."

Mom must have decided it wasn't worth a fight. She moved in to give me a hug, even though I'm often uncomfortable with the gesture. I figured it would get her out of here quicker though, if I reciprocated.

Dad and I don't really hug. Instead, he handed me a fistful of cash. "If you need anything for the room, charge it on your credit card. I mean anything."

I smiled, thanking him.

My parents were gone pretty quickly. I didn't follow them out in the hall to watch them leave. I was close enough to home that I'd be seeing them regularly. Plus, I didn't want to see if my dad punched any of the boys loitering in the hallway as he departed.

After they were gone, I turned to Paris and Brittany expectantly. "So we don't know who else is in here with us?"

"No," Paris said. "We were going to wait until everyone was here to choose beds, but I'm ready to start putting stuff together."

"Me, too," I agreed. "If she doesn't like what bed she gets, tough. She should have gotten here sooner."

Paris couldn't help but smile. I could tell she was thinking the same thing. For her part, Brittany still looked doubtful.

"Come on," I prodded her. "It will be fine."

We all left our stuff in the common room – which was sparsely furnished with four desks and nothing else. We all wandered into the bedroom and looked at each other expectantly.

"Anyone have any preference?" Paris asked.

I jumped right in. "I'd prefer a top bunk." I'm not shy – and we were going to be stuck with these beds for nine months.

"I'd prefer a bottom bunk," Paris said. "Why don't we take the beds on the right?"

"Sounds good to me."

We both turned and looked at Brittany. "You can pick whichever bed you want."

Even though she was still nervous, Brittany ultimately took the top bunk on the left side of the room near the window.

Paris and I were both eyeing the room with the same idea. Paris voiced it first. "If we move the beds end to end against the far wall, we can fit all four desks in here, too. That would allow us to make the main room just for entertainment."

"I think that's a great idea," I said enthusiastically.

"What if the other girl doesn't like that idea?" Brittany was going to be a pain. I could tell right away. She needed to loosen up – and quick.

"She'll live."

Paris laughed and nodded.

We immediately got to work. With all three of us working, it didn't take long to get things in shape. Paris and I already had our beds made, including alarm clocks and fans in place, while Brittany was still trying to find her sheets. It didn't surprise me when she pulled out a boring set of floral bedding. I'd bought Star Wars sheets and Paris had a tie-dyed set.

Paris and I each hauled in our suitcases and started to unpack. There were two different closets, one on each side of the room. Paris and I took the one closet and quickly managed to stow all of our clothes without a problem. Ironically, we had a lot of the same shoes. Converse had obviously made a lot of money off the two of us.

When we were finished, Brittany was still working on making her bed. I wanted to laugh at her attempt to do hospital corners, but I let it go. I didn't think this was the best way to create harmony in the room.

Paris and I walked out into the common room and looked around. Luckily, Paris had the foresight to bring a television – but other than that, we had no furniture.

"Want to go shopping?"

"Will your dad mind?"

"No. He expects it."

"Maybe we should wait and see what our other roommate brings?" Brittany said.

That was probably a good idea, so Paris and I sat down on the floor in the main room to get to know one another. Brittany remained unpacking in the bedroom, but she answered whatever questions we tossed her way.

In short order, I found out that Brittany was an only child like me, but Paris was one of ten kids who ranged in age from thirty to five. I figured her parents must have been busy. They sounded like free-love hippies, though. I was cautiously optimistic that Paris and I would be good friends.

About two hours into the conversation, the door of our room opened and a redheaded girl stood uncertainly in the doorway.

"Hi," I greeted her warmly, introducing myself to her. Paris followed suit. For her part, Brittany seemed to be hiding in the bedroom. I guess she was worried there might be some sort of fallout from the whole bed thing.

"I'm Tara," the redhead said, pulling a suitcase behind her.

"We already picked beds," I offered. I didn't offer to change the situation if she didn't like it. I wasn't feeling that magnanimous.

"That's fine," she said. "I'm not picky."

Brittany seemed to visibly relax in the doorway when she heard that and quickly showed Tara what we'd done with the bedroom.

"That's a great idea," Tara said looking around. "You guys have done a lot of work."

"It really wasn't that much work," I answered. "It just seemed to make more sense to do it now rather than wait until we'd all made our beds and everything."

Tara agreed. She started unpacking her stuff right away. She didn't seem to have a problem fitting in with everyone else. Despite Brittany being uptight, I didn't think this was a bad room configuration -- as far as personalities went anyway.

Everyone continued to gossip.

Brittany, it turns out, was from a high-class portion of Oakland County (a suburb of Detroit). Paris was from a small town about an hour north of the city and Tara was from a minuscule town about an hour east of Covenant College. We all had vastly different backgrounds, I noticed. I guess that's what college is about, though.

Tara was still seeing her high school boyfriend and he lived back home – so she said she'd probably be spending a lot of her weekends back with her parents so she could see him. I couldn't help but wonder how long that would last – but I wisely kept my mouth shut.

Paris also had a boyfriend. He was at Covenant, though, and he was two years older than us. I figured that was going to make getting beer so much easier.

I then told them about my boyfriend, Will. Will and I had been together since I was fourteen years old. He was from a small town about fifteen minutes from the town I had grown up in. It had two stoplights. He was going into his junior year at Covenant. If I'm being truthful, that's probably another reason I opted for Covenant – I just didn't want him to know that.

Despite the fact that we'd been together for four years, Will and I had taken a pragmatic approach to our relationship. We were together, but we weren't fanatical about it when I was still in high school and he was in college. I had a feeling he'd had a few flings – but I really didn't want to know about them. For my part, I'd taken a good friend to prom and there might have been a little messing around. Nothing major, though.

When I told Will that I would be going to Covenant, he was excited. We'd agreed that we were going to give monogamy a shot. I figured we'd start that tomorrow. I was kind of interested in meeting the guys out in the hallway.

I opened the door – figuring if anyone wanted to meet us, this was the way to go about the process -- and Paris pulled out a deck of cards.

"You know how to play euchre?"

I smiled. I knew I was going to like Paris.

Brittany and Tara had finished unpacking at this point. It may have been uneventful, but it was the perfect night of bonding.

If this is college, I thought, then this is going to be a great year.

I couldn't know how truly wrong I would be.

2 TWO

The next morning I didn't wake up until almost 11 a.m. I felt Paris stir in the bottom bunk about the same time consciousness claimed me. Our late night gab session had gone until almost 3 a.m. – but it had been a great way for all of us to get to know one another.

I rolled over and saw that Brittany was not only up but had made her bed. I hoped she didn't expect the same from me. I had no intention of making my bed again until I returned home in the spring. I couldn't see into the bottom bunk, but I had a feeling Tara was up, too. It looked like Paris and I were going to be the late sleepers.

I climbed out of the bunk, muttering something unintelligible to Paris as I moved toward the door into the common room – which was shut. Paris responded with something equally as garbled. Somehow I was getting the impression that the right side of the room was going to be grumpy in the morning. That was fine by me. The less someone talked to me when I first got up, the better.

When I went into the empty common room, I noticed that neither Brittany nor Tara were there. I couldn't muster up the energy to care as I climbed into the shower – where I let the never-ending stream of scalding water wake me up for the next twenty minutes. When I exited the bathroom, Paris went in behind me and closed the door. We still hadn't exchanged morning pleasantries.

I went back into the bedroom to dress and put my makeup on. I dried my hair and hastily tied a purple bandana over it as I donned a tank top and cutoffs.

Paris took less time to get ready than I did – and I couldn't help but be a little jealous at how good she looked even though she hadn't put on a stitch of makeup or done her hair.

"Want breakfast?" One of us had finally spoken.

"Sure," I answered. "Although, it's technically lunch now."

We made our way down to the main floor. Our dorms were on the fifth floor and we both wordlessly took the stairs down. I had a feeling it would be a different situation when it came time to climb back up – but that was something I'd tackle later.

When we reached the dining area, we both handed our school IDs over to the girl at the door. She swiped them through the machine without even bothering to look up at us and make sure our faces matched our pictures. I guess lunchroom fraud wasn't a big deal.

Once inside the cafeteria, Paris and I both plodded to the line to check out the food situation. You hear horror stories about college food – but it looked pretty good to me. I settled for chicken fingers and fries. I noticed Paris got the same thing. I was glad to see she wasn't a health nut.

Once we both had our trays, we turned to decide where to sit.

"Paris, Zoe, over here."

We both turned to see Brittany and Tara seated at a table a few feet away. We made our way to the table and sat down with them.

"We were wondering if you two were going to ever get up," Brittany's voice was like nails on a chalkboard. That was definitely a sound I wasn't going to want to hear when I had a hangover.

Tara seemed to read my mind because she hid her smirk behind a cup of coffee. Rather than saying something snarky, I shoved the straw from my pop into my mouth instead. It was too early to be bitchy.

"Did you sleep well?" Brittany was not to be deterred.

"As compared to what?" Apparently Paris didn't like being around bubbly people when she first got up either.

Brittany looked confused. "As compared to sleeping badly."

Sarcasm was going to be lost on this girl -- that much was obvious. "We slept fine."

The conversation jumped from theme to theme after that, with all four of us discussing what classes we had signed up for and our need to go book shopping at some point. We all had our first classes on Monday. Since it was Friday, we figured we had plenty of time to go and buy our books.

"Let's just go Sunday," Paris said, dipping her chicken fingers into a big pile of ketchup.

"That's the day before classes," Brittany frowned.

"So?"

"Well, don't you want to start reading them right away?"

Paris and I both froze with food in our mouths. I swallowed, trying to buy time before answering. I should have bought more time.

"You were a nerd in high school weren't you?"

Brittany looked hurt. "What's that supposed to mean?"

"Who would want to read textbooks before they have to?"

"Someone that loves to learn," Brittany was becoming a little shrill. "I don't want to fail out."

"You're not going to fail out," Tara soothed, shooting me a dirty look for getting Brittany worked up. I sensed a divide forming in the room. Paris must have, too.

"I don't think that's what Zoe was saying," she said. "I think she was just pointing out that it might be a waste of time to read the text-books before hand – especially if we're only covering certain chapters in class."

Nice save. Although that's not really what I was saying.

Brittany seemed to relax at Paris' explanation. "I never thought of that."

"I just don't want to think about school when we have the weekend in front of us," I said.

"What are we going to do?" Uh-oh, Brittany was a "we" person.

Paris seemed nonplussed by the development, too. "I don't know," she said carefully. "I'm going to a party at my boyfriend's tonight."

"A party? With beer?"

I smirked at Paris as I took another sip of my Diet Coke. I wondered how she was going to handle this.

"Yes, there will be beer there."

"Are you going to drink it?"

"Yes." Paris turned to me. "You're coming, right?"

I got the feeling she didn't want to be stuck alone with Brittany.

"Sure," I said with a laugh. "Will and I agreed we weren't going to see each other this weekend so I could get to know you guys and he could party with his frat brothers."

"Which frat is he in?"

I shrugged. "I don't know. I think it's Alpha Chi, or something like that."

"That's the best frat on campus," Brittany said knowingly.

"Really? What scale are they grading on?"

Brittany looked confused again. I was starting to think she was socially retarded. God, I hope she wasn't home schooled.

"The guys in Alpha Chi are supposed to be very academically minded," she said.

"How do you know that?"

"When I stopped to get a brochure on Delta Zeta they told me," she said.

Paris and I exchanged looks.

"You're going to rush a sorority?" Paris asked. She looked as worried as I felt.

"Yes," Brittany was excited. "Probably not until next semester, though. I want to get settled before I rush a sorority."

"Why would you want to rush a sorority?" Whoops, did I just ask that out loud?

"Why wouldn't I?"

"Why would you?"

"Why wouldn't I?"

Paris stepped in. "I think what Zoe means is, why do you feel the need to rush a sorority? Can't you make friends on your own?" Yeah, that was so much better than how I would have phrased it.

"Yes, but a sorority isn't about friends ... it's about sisters."

Uh, gag me.

Brittany must have seen the look of distaste cross my face.

"I notice you don't have the same problem with fraternities," she sniffed.

"I think fraternities are equally useless," I offered. "It's just that I think the guys go into fraternities so they have easy access to women for sex and older guys on hand to buy beer."

Paris snorted out her laughter. "I would agree with that."

"And why do you think girls go into sororities?"

Now this was a dangerous question – and Brittany didn't look like she was going to let it go. In a typical situation, I would try to deflect. Brittany didn't seem like the type of girl who could be distracted, though. I decided to be honest.

"I think girls – some girls," I corrected myself hastily. "I think that maybe they join sororities to buy friends."

There it was.

Brittany looked offended. Tara looked interested in her reaction. And Paris? She looked like she was fighting to keep from laughing out loud.

"Why would I need to buy friends?"

"I didn't say you needed to buy friends," I offered lamely. This conversation was getting uncomfortable. "I just think it's weird that you would want to go into a sorority where you have to pay money and they make you do lame things and then they want you to agree to essentially think just like them."

I should have stopped there. I didn't.

"It's like a cult," I finished.

Paris coughed to cover up her laughter. Brittany looked furious.

"That's not true," she argued vehemently. "Sororities are about making lifelong contacts and friends. It's about networking."

"Why do you need to pay to make contacts? Why can't you just make contacts on your own? And why do you have to do it with a group whose whole purpose is to keep out other people? To only let in those who are desirable in their eyes?"

I was on a roll now.

"And who decides who is desirable? If they don't like your haircut, are they going to keep you out? If they don't think you dress appropriately does that reflect badly on you? If you prefer *True Blood* over *The Vampire Diaries* are they going to blackball you?"

Yep, I should have stopped while I was ahead.

Brittany launched into a lengthy diatribe describing the merits of sororities and how I was a bigot. Quite frankly, I tuned her out. Paris was shaking with silent laughter beside me.

For my part, I concentrated on my lunch while trying to feign interest on whatever Brittany was whining about now. Finally, I realized there was a lull in the conversation. I realized everyone at the table was looking at me. "What?"

Paris bit her lower lip to keep from smiling. "Brittany just wanted to know what you were wearing to the party tonight."

"That's not what I asked her," Brittany argued.

"Yes, it is," Paris replied.

"No, it's not," she said.

"Yes, it is," Tara stressed.

Brittany decided to try one more time. "No, it's not."

"Yes, it is!" Both Tara and Paris were done with the conversation.

I smiled sweetly at Brittany in an attempt to placate her. "It's still warm out, so I figured I'd just wear a pair of cutoffs and a top."

Brittany seemed to be waging an internal debate. Finally, she just gave in and nodded. "Sounds good."

Something told me the sorority debate wasn't over yet.

3 THREE

After lunch, we decided to go shopping for some furniture for the common room. No one wanted to sit on the floor anymore – especially one that didn't have a rug.

There weren't a lot of places to choose from – especially on a college budget – so we all settled for Meijer.

I was a little apprehensive about how things were going to go – especially given how uptight Brittany was in general – but everything went smoothly.

We got a simple rug for the middle of the room, a small refrigerator, a wicker chair and a futon couch. It wasn't great furniture – but it was comfortable. I knew my dad wouldn't care about how much money I spent either – he was good that way.

After transporting all the furniture back to the dorm and assembling things, everyone started making plans for the party later that night.

Since she was so nervous, Brittany showered first. While she was in the bathroom, Tara informed us that Brittany had already showered, but she wanted to look 'especially good' in case there were hot guys in attendance.

Paris and I found the situation funny, but Tara warned us about pushing Brittany too far.

"I think she's one of those girls who's so uptight that she could snap in the middle of the night and kills us all," Tara admitted.

"She wouldn't kill us," I disagreed. "She might cut all our hair off or something ... or try to use the Epilady on us ... but she wouldn't kill us."

Paris sat on the floor with us and dealt out a hand of three-handed euchre – not as much fun as regular euchre – but distracting enough to hold our attention. "What that girl needs is to get laid."

I didn't disagree with the sentiment. The night before, Brittany had said she'd slept with one guy one time but didn't like it. Now she wanted to wait until she was in love.

"That was a lie," Tara agreed.

"Nobody doesn't like it," I said.

Paris smirked at me.

"What?"

"I'm just picturing you with a whip," she said.

"Why?"

"You're too bossy not to be the one in control."

This was true.

"Sex can still be good even without an orgasm," Tara offered.

I felt sorry for her. "That's a load of crap."

"It really is," Paris said.

After finishing the game, Tara, Paris, and I all went into the bedroom to get ready.

Since we weren't as over-protected as Brittany, none of us were as worried about getting ready. I kept on the cutoffs I'd been wearing all day and switched out the tank top with a simple black V-neck. I then tied a flannel shirt around my waist in case I got cold later. I finished the outfit off with my Nike flip-flops. Cute, but comfortable. We had about a half a mile walk to get to the party.

Paris put on a pair of denim capris and an Old Navy T-Shirt. I could tell she didn't care about getting dressed up either. She finished off her outfit with a pair of cute boat shoes that I made a mental note to borrow at a later date. We'd already compared shoe size, and were tickled to find out we both wore a size nine. That was going to expand the Converse selection by quite a bit for both of us.

Tara dressed in simple jean shorts and a Detroit Tigers' T-shirt. She put on Chuck Taylor shoes without socks – something I generally frown upon – but still managed to look cute.

We were all ready and waiting for Brittany – who seemed to be in a blind panic.

"I don't know what to wear," she admitted.

We tried to tell her to wear anything she was comfortable in. When she came out in dress pants and a blazer, Paris disgustedly followed her back into the bedroom.

"Haven't you ever been to a party?"

Fifteen minutes later, they came back out into the common room. Paris had forced Brittany into a pair of cargo pants and a T-shirt – and Brittany was complaining bitterly.

"I don't feel comfortable in this," she argued.

"Well, if you wear the other outfit, people are going to think you're a narc," I offered.

"What do you mean a narc?"

"Like you're there to dime them out to the cops because they're smoking pot," I explained.

"Is there going to be pot there?" Brittany looked panicked again.

Paris was just annoyed at this point.

"Yes, there's going to be pot there and you're going to be fine. Other people smoking pot isn't going to kill you."

"I know that," Brittany scoffed. "It's a gateway drug, though, and if I get a contact high, I could be date raped."

"We won't let you be date raped," Tara soothed, looking to me for backup. I didn't want her to get raped, but I thought a little sex might dislodge that big old stick .... Tara kicked me pointedly.

"We won't let you get date raped," I reluctantly agreed.

The walk to Paris' boyfriend's apartment – which was several blocks off campus – seemed a lot longer than it should have. Brittany was getting more and more amped up as we made the trek.

"Do you think there will be guys there?"

"It's being thrown by my boyfriend and his roommates – so yes, there will be guys there."

"Are they hot?"

"I've never met them," Paris admitted.

"What if they're not hot?"

"Then definitely don't sleep with them," I suggested.

"You're not helping," Paris growled.

I didn't tell her that I wasn't trying to help.

When we got to the apartment complex, I followed Paris up the stairs. She didn't bother knocking, pushing open the door and frowning slightly as she heard what music was playing. "I hate Nickelback," she grumbled.

"Who doesn't?"

Paris made her way across the crowded apartment to greet a blonde guy who was holding court around the keg. He wasn't quite what I was expecting. Where Paris was exotic looking and beautiful, this guy – I think she said his name was Mike – was an example of all things ordinary. He had curly blonde hair, big glasses and was about twenty pounds overweight.

"He must be good in bed," I said to Tara.

Tara smiled at me. "You're awful judgmental."

"I'm shallow," I corrected her. "Paris is too pretty for him. It won't last."

Tara stifled a giggle. "You have no filter."

"Nope."

"I kind of find it refreshing," she said.

"It will get old pretty quick," I admitted.

"Probably."

After being introduced to Mike and his roommates – all who looked like they were in their mid-20s and tried get a sneak peek down my V-neck – I pumped a glass of beer and wandered out onto the balcony to get away from the cloud of pot smoke that was making it hard to breathe in the other room.

I'm not a pot hater – in fact I like to partake a little too often, if I'm being honest – but I never smoke with people I don't know. I'm nothing if not safety oriented.

There was only one other person out on the balcony – and he was dressed all in black.

I sat down in one of the plastic chairs that was positioned slightly behind him and eyed him carefully. I'm not a big fan of the Goth scene – and this guy screamed Goth. He was wearing black cargo pants, a black T-shirt and black Doc Marten boots. Luckily, it didn't look like he was wearing makeup.

Most Goth fans weren't as ripped as him, though, or as tan. I couldn't help but notice his darker coloring. The tan looked nice with his tropically blessed skin.

He must have felt me looking at him because he slowly turned to face me. It was then that I noticed that his face was as good as his body. High cheek bones, dark brown eyes, and a hint of a crease in his cheeks that I was almost positive housed dimples. All this was framed with shoulder length black hair that screamed "cool" instead of "1980s reject."

He was hot.

Still, I'd seen hot guys before. I wasn't going to fall over myself for some guy on a balcony. I mean, I was in a committed relationship with ... Christ, what was that guy's name again?

Mr. Sexy in the corner offered me a warm smile – yep, I was right, he had dimples -- as he looked me up and down. I tried to act cool. He may be hot, but I definitely wasn't interested. Since that usually backfires on me, this time was no different, and instead of nonchalantly sipping on my beer I coughed as it went down the wrong hole.

Mr. Sexy smiled as he saw me sputter.

"Are you alright?"

Okay, like any other self-respecting woman, I'm turned on by a nice accent. South African accents are the best, but this guy's Latin accent was a nice second.

"I'm fine," I said once I regained my bearings. I was mortally embarrassed, but I was fine.

"I'm Rafael," he held his hand out in greeting.

I'm not someone who usually shakes people's hands, but something compelled me to this time. I think it was the small voice in my mind that was wondering what he would look like naked. The minute I touched his hand it was like nothing in the world existed besides him.

He stepped in even closer – invading my personal space.

Okay, it wasn't so cute anymore.

He peered deep into my eyes, clasping my hand with both of his and stared hard into my face.

"And you are?"

"Oh," my cheeks burned red in embarrassment. Thank God it was nighttime. I was flustered, but I hadn't lost sense of myself. "Zoe."

"Zoe what?"

"Zoe Lake."

Rafael seemed to take the information in, but he didn't respond. I was slowly starting to regain my wits, though. I pulled my hand out of his and took a step back, narrowing my eyes dangerously at him.

"What's your deal?"

"What?" Rafael looked surprised.

"What's your deal?" I repeated.

"I don't know what you mean?" Rafael unleashed the dimples again.

Finally, I got it. It was like my mind was climbing out of a hole. "You're used to women swooning, I get that, but it's not okay to invade my personal space like that."

Rafael looked momentarily flummoxed. "What do you mean?"

"It's like *Dirty Dancing*," I gestured. "This is my dance space. That is your dance space."

Rafael openly frowned now.

"I don't know what you mean."

"Listen, you're cute, I'll give you that," I acknowledged. "You're no Chris Hemsworth, though, so you might not want to crowd people."

"Who is Chris Hemsworth?" The accent was still intoxicating.

Playing dumb, however, wasn't. "You know, Thor?"

"The Norse god?"

"No, the actor who played the Norse god?" Maybe he wasn't playing dumb.

Rafael still looked confused.

"It doesn't matter," I said, waving my hand dismissively. "I was just trying to explain to you that I'm not impressed by your dimples."

Rafael didn't seem convinced.

I stood my ground, not returning his smile.

Rafael started to move closer. "I think you just need to relax."

I took a step back. "Thanks, I'm good."

Rafael furrowed his eyebrows in confusion. I started to wonder if maybe there was a language barrier or something.

"No interested ... comprende?"

Now Rafael looked irritated. "I'm not stupid."

"Then stop acting like it," I snapped.

Rafael pulled away in obvious irritation this time. He started to move back toward the apartment before stopping abruptly and turning back to me.

"Be careful going home."

I thought that was a weird thing to say to someone you'd just met. "Is that a threat?" This guy was unbelievable.

"No."

Rafael slid back into the apartment, shutting the door behind him as he went.

It took me a full thirty seconds to recover and follow him inside. I wasn't sure what his deal was, but I wanted to just forget about it and have some fun. That was what we had come here for, after all.

I rejoined Paris by the keg, but kept a keen eye out for Rafael. To my relief, it appeared he had left. Okay, maybe I was a little disappointed, too.

I silently admonished myself for even thinking about him. After all, Will and I were finally on the same page – and in the same place – I wasn't going to throw that away for some random guy. No matter how hot he was. Or how sexy that accent was. Or how great he looked in that T-shirt. I reminded myself he was creepy, too, because he was definitely creepy.

"Did you even hear me?"

"What?" I turned to Paris confused.

"I said that Brittany seems to have gotten over her panic about meeting guys."

I turned my attention in the direction Paris was looking only to find Brittany drinking from a red plastic cup and hanging on every word as one of Mike's roommates talked to her. She looked tipsy – and easy. I hoped that wasn't her way of flirting. Paris and I were going to have to give her lessons.

"We're going to have to watch her," I said.

Paris agreed, nodding silently, and slipping a lock of her long brown hair behind her ear.

"She's one of those girls who's going to lose her virginity finally and go nuts and sleep with everyone to make up for what she's been missing."

Paris nodded again.

"Who is that guy?"

"I have no idea."

"He looks like Pee Wee Herman."

"Just be glad we're not in an adult movie theater." Paris was still eyeing Brittany and her new friend warily.

I nodded my silent assent as I took another drink of beer. The one good thing about Brittany's antics? I'd forgotten all about Rafael.

What? I totally had.

4 FOUR

Hangovers are a funny thing. When you wake up with them in high school, you try to hide them. When you wake up with them in college, though, there's no need.

Luckily for me, I hadn't over imbibed the night before. From the groans I could hear from Brittany's bed the next morning, though, it didn't sound like she was so lucky.

While still lying in my bunk and contemplating how badly I wanted to get something to drink to ease my cotton mouth, I heard Brittany vault out of her bunk and rush out of the room. Two seconds later you could hear the door to the bathroom slam shut.

I could hear – and feel – Paris start laughing in the bunk below me.

"We should have kept a better eye on her," I finally said to no one in particular.

"She learned a valuable lesson," I heard Tara say sagely from her bunk – which was the first inclination I had that she was awake, too.

Paris stirred and climbed out of her bed. When she stood up and met my eyes I could see she had a fantastic case of bedhead. I smiled to myself – but Paris caught me trying to hide it.

"Your hair doesn't look any better," she said.

I could believe that.

Tara, Paris, and I struggled out to the living area where we met Brittany as she stumbled out of the bathroom. "I hate you people," she mumbled.

"You'll feel better after breakfast," I informed her.

Brittany was looking a little green again.

"Yeah. Eggs and sausage, tons of grease, hangover food extraordinaire." I couldn't decide if Paris was trying to help or hurt the situation. Sausage did sound good, though.

An hour later, we'd all showered and changed. We went down for breakfast – well, brunch actually – and discussed the evening before. For my part, I decided not to mention Rafael – at least not to everyone. I didn't know what I'd say anyway. He hadn't actually done anything.

"Anyone up for going and getting our books now?"

Paris looked at me in surprise. "I thought you wanted to put it off like I did?"

"I do, but I figure we're not going to do anything else for the next couple of hours anyways, so we might as well get it out of the way," I sipped my pop and looked at Brittany contemplatively for a second. "Plus, Brittany looks like she's been reincarnated as a dirty sponge so she's probably not going to be up for doing anything tonight and will enjoy the company of her textbooks."

Everyone agreed and we decided to make the walk to the University Center, or UC, to get our shopping done. We'd all returned to the room long enough to get our class lists. We compared them as we walked.

"Ooh, we have astronomy together," Paris actually seemed excited.

I didn't know how excited I was. I just wanted something that wasn't too gross to complete my science requirement. I had a feeling that's why Paris signed up, too. She was an art major. Cutting open a frog didn't seem like something that was going to be in her wheelhouse.

When we got to the UC, we were happy to discover that the bookstore wasn't too crowded. The good news is that three of my five textbooks were available for my ereader so that meant less heavy lifting. Unfortunately, I had to buy textbooks for my math and astronomy classes. Still, it was better than it could have been.

Paris only had to buy the astronomy class book. Brittany, however, bought textbooks for all her classes. When we saw her carrying two large bags full of books over to us, Paris and I exchanged a curious glance.

"They're not available digitally?" I asked.

"I don't like digital books."

"Why?"

"What do you mean why? I like a real textbook where I can underline stuff."

"You can underline stuff with an ereader, too."

"Not with a colored highlighter."

Well, you can't argue with that logic. Brittany found herself distracted by the sweatshirts. For my part, I decided I needed a Coke to drive away the remnants of my hangover.

I made my way over to the refrigerated section and found what I was looking for. I slid the door shut after I made my selection and turned around only to find myself running into a wall that was apparently some guy's chest. I actually wasn't sure at first. It was far too big to belong to a normal guy.

"Sorry," I sputtered trying to take a step back and banging my head against the refrigerator.

The chest belonged to an extremely tall man – like six-foot three-inches tall – who took a step back to give me a chance to recover myself. As I regained my senses I realized – even though he'd moved back slightly – he was still a little too close for my comfort.

"Are you alright?" The voice that came from the behemoth couldn't possibly be human – or normal. It sounded like it belonged to a giant or something – like Fezzik in *The Princess Bride* without that weird lisp thing he had.

"I'm fine," I grumbled. I didn't like feeling penned in.

"Here, let me see," the guy reached his extremely large hands toward my head.

Without thinking, I slapped them away. "I said I was fine."

I finally got a glimpse at the head attached to the wall of chest and sucked in a quick breath. It was pretty impressive – well, as far as heads go. No dimples and dark skin, but a full head of wavy black hair and some really intense brown eyes.

Did Covenant grow these guys on trees or something? This is just ridiculous.

"I'm not going to hurt you," the guy rumbled.

I felt a little ridiculous for overreacting – especially since I realized he was hot – so I tried to offer him a friendly smile as an apology.

"No, you just took me by surprise," I said quietly. Internally, I was adding that he also almost knocked me senseless – but I doubted that would be a good topic of conversation to open with.

The wall of muscles with the great hair smiled down at me. I couldn't help but notice that, even though he didn't have dimples, his eyes crinkled at the corner when he smiled and it made him all the more appealing. *Cripes, I must be in heat or something.*

"I'm Aric, with an A," he said, pushing his hand out to me in greeting.

What is it with people shaking hands? That whole process annoyed me. Still, I didn't want to offend him. I placed my hand – which seemed dainty – into it and couldn't help but smile back. I felt a little goofy for some reason.

"I'm Zoe."

"Nice to meet you, Zoe. Where are you from?"

Now, here's the thing, I'm not a shut-in or anything. I don't go around volunteering personal information about myself either, though.

"Oh, a small town up north. About an hour from Traverse City."
I was purposely vague.

Aric narrowed his eyes. I sensed he wanted to ask more but
wisely took a step back.

"I'm from Alpena."

I bit my tongue so I wouldn't unleash the sentence that had come
to mind when he mentioned Alpena. "That's nice." What I really
wanted to say amounted to 'who cares,' but I fought the urge to be
mean. It was a hard battle.

"Are you a freshman?"

"Umm, yeah."

"I'm a sophomore."

"Really? You look older."

"Is that a compliment?"

I shrugged. It was really just a statement.

"I'm twenty-two. I took some time off before coming to school,"
he explained. This guy was a major over-sharer. For all he knew, I
could be some crazy stalker – yet here he was telling me his life story.

"Good for you." Really, what else do you say to that?

"Are you here alone?" I noticed his dark eyes dart around the
store. I could tell he was trying to get a look at what kind of people I
hung out with. It made me sort of nervous.

"I'm here with my roommates."

"Oh, have you known them a long time?"

Now why did that matter? Luckily I was saved from answering.
Paris had picked that moment to come up and join us.

"Brittany is buying out the school spirit supplies." She didn't
sound happy.

"She's not decorating with that stuff," I warned. Covenant's
colors were red and gold. I hated both colors.

"You tell her that."

Paris finally noticed I wasn't alone. She wasn't very observant.
She smiled at Aric, though. It was hard not to.

"I'm Paris."

Aric introduced himself, greeting Paris warmly. Still, I couldn't shake the feeling that he was a little disappointed we'd been interrupted. Or maybe that was wishful thinking on my part.

"So, did you guys go to high school together?" More questions. I tried to give Paris a silent signal not to answer him, but she was oblivious.

"No, we just met two days ago," she answered.

"It's good that you like each other."

"Yeah, it would suck if I was stuck in a room with three Brittanys."

Well, that mental image was going to give me nightmares. I shuddered as I shook it off.

"So, what dorm do you live in?"

I mentally sent Paris the universal "don't answer that" vibe. She didn't get it. She happily told Aric where we lived. I wanted to strangle her.

"Good to know," Aric smiled. The smile wasn't directed at Paris, though. It was directed at me. Great. How was I going to explain to Will about the new guy following me everywhere?

"Is it just the two of you?" Aric asked. He really had no end to his questions.

"No, our other two roommates are here, too," Paris said. She pointed silently to Brittany. Aric followed her finger and I could tell he was fighting the urge to laugh out loud at the pile of sweatshirts in front of her.

"Who else?"

Paris looked around quizzically. "I don't know where Tara went."

I found myself looking around for Tara, too. It was like she had just disappeared. "She wouldn't have left without us ... ." Actually, I had no idea what Tara would do. I didn't really know her at all.

Paris looked doubtful. "No, she would have at least said something."

Aric regarded us sternly. "Bonded a lot have you?"

"Just with each other," Paris admitted.

I tried to peer around Aric. It was a monumental task, though. He was big. For a second I couldn't help but wonder what he looked like without his sweatshirt on. I'd run into him so I knew that wasn't flab under there. He was hard as a rock – and built like a truck, I was almost certain.

"There she is," I finally caught sight of her red hair.

Tara was outside. I could just get a glimpse of her through the window. She was gesturing wildly – and she didn't look happy. I couldn't see whom she was talking to. She stopped long enough to point – and her finger was aimed directly at me. She seemed to notice that we were all looking at her because she quickly tried to disguise her motions.

Whoever she was talking with walked away from her quickly. All I could make out is that it was a boy and he had close-cut blonde hair. He was gone too quickly to see anything else.

Tara made her way back into the store and smiled brightly at us. I couldn't help but think it was a little fake. She walked over to us laughing. "I went to high school with him," she explained.

"Really? You should have come in and introduced him to us," Paris seemed genuinely interested.

"Oh, I went to high school with him, but I didn't like him," she explained. "He wanted to invite us to a party."

"I don't think Brittany is up for another party," I answered. Paris nodded her silent assent. For his part, Aric didn't seem to be listening. He was still watching the spot where Tara had been arguing with her high school classmate. He looked thoughtful.

"Yeah, I don't know what I'm up for tonight either," Tara said with a laugh.

Paris had obviously dismissed the argument. I was suspicious by nature, but even I didn't blame her for wanting to get away from high school 'friends.' That was why I had come here in the first place.

Aric finally seemed to snap to attention. He smiled down at all of us – letting his eyes linger on me a little longer than everyone else. "It was nice meeting you all."

"You, too," Paris and Tara said. They both looked a little dreamy.

Aric turned to me expectantly. "Bye," I said with false bravado.

Aric smiled a small half smile to himself as he regarded me. I could tell he wanted to call me on my attitude, but he wisely refrained from any such action.

"I'll see you around."

"Doubtful."

I thought I'd said it under my breath, but apparently he'd heard me. He turned around briefly before exiting. "You can count on it."

Despite myself, I felt a little thrill of anticipation. Seriously, what is wrong with me?

5 FIVE

Sunday morning I woke up with a mixed sense of dread and excitement.

This was the last day off before classes started. While I was excited to be in college – academia had never really been my thing. Still, I only had five classes – and none of them were gym -- so I was already better off than high school.

As a group, we'd all decided to stay in and just play cards and gab the night before. Brittany was still recovering. I could only hope she'd work up a tolerance. I didn't want to think of her being such a light-weight the entire year. That was going to make babysitting her a real task.

We all went down to breakfast together as a group – where Brittany proceeded to explain to all of us the benefits of a gluten-free diet. I was only half listening – but I realized quickly that was going to eliminate every cereal I liked – so that obviously wasn't going to happen.

After breakfast, we returned to our room but left the door open. I figured it was time to get to know some of our floor mates better.

The guys across the hall came to introduce themselves pretty quickly. There were two Ricks, a Greg and a Milton. Yeah, his parents obviously sucked.

They seemed like nice guys – but none of them exactly screamed 'brainiac' to me. I think they were mostly here for the parties and women – which was fine with me.

Rick No. 1 sat down next to me and tried to engage me in a conversation. Of the two Ricks, he was clearly the more intelligent of the two, but I was pretty sure that wasn't saying much. I answered most of his questions in a non-committal way. I was friendly, not gregarious.

For their part, Brittany and Milton seemed to be enjoying a friendly chat. It didn't surprise me in the slightest.

Before I knew it, though, it was lunchtime and we all decided to go down to the cafeteria together. I figured that expanding our group could only benefit me – mostly because Brittany was going to be so high maintenance.

As we traversed the cafeteria with our trays, I realized that Tara had been largely quiet today. She'd been friendly and nice to the guys, but when she thought no one was looking, she was lost in contemplation. I couldn't help but wonder if it had something to do with the guy we had seen her with at the UC the day before. I didn't ask, though. It was none of my business.

Toward the tail end of lunch, a tall boy with long hair made his way over to the table. His hair was blonde – so blonde it almost looked like an ashy gray. He had warm brown eyes and he carried a skateboard. I smiled in spite of myself. A hipster carrying a skateboard indoors could only mean one thing: pothead.

Brittany smiled when she saw the boy approach our table. It was a watery smile, though, and I could tell she was concerned about seeing him.

"Mark," she squealed, yes squealed, and threw her arms around him. It seemed like an extreme reaction for someone who looked surprised to see him a few minutes before and embarrassed to see him a minute after that.

For his part, Mark seemed surprised by the greeting as well. Still, he hugged her back before returning his gaze to everyone at the table.

Brittany was bubbly as she introduced Mark. "We went to high school together ... although we didn't really hang around in the same circles."

I smiled to myself. I could bet what circles Brittany ran around with – were the same circles I secretly dreamed of starting on fire when I was bored in detention. Mark, though, I bet he ran around in similar circles to me – and I bet those circles were often drowned in a haze of hemp.

Mark must have sensed a kinship with me, too, because when Brittany asked him if he wanted to join us he immediately moved to the side of the table Paris and I were sitting on and wedged himself between us. I couldn't help but laugh.

Paris, Mark, and I enjoyed some idle chatter for a while. Paris asked him about his skateboard – even being so bold as to question him about whether or not she could ride it.

I thought that was pretty brave. Most skateboard aficionados don't let anyone touch their ride.

Mark was either baked or laid back, as he acquiesced almost immediately.

"You want to come try, too?" He seemed eager for me to agree.

Interestingly enough, I did. I have negative balance on roller blades, but maybe a skateboard would be different. I could ski, after all. Of course, when you fall while skiing it's usually in a big soft drift of snow. Pavement is a different thing.

Paris, Mark, and I said goodbye to everyone at the table. I couldn't help but notice a dark look emanating from Brittany as she watched us go. For a minute I wondered if she had a crush on Mark. I realized pretty quickly that probably wasn't it. Still, I couldn't figure out why she was suddenly so hostile.

Pushing the thoughts out of my mind, Paris, Mark, and I went to the sidewalk area behind the dorm. There were a couple of blankets spread out in the grassy knoll being occupied by a few couples – but for the most part the area was empty.

Mark gave us a quick tutorial on how to balance ourselves on the board before he nervously handed his pride and joy – which I noticed had Smurf decals on the undercarriage – over to Paris.

I was surprised. Paris didn't seem like the athletic type to me. She quickly caught on to the skateboard, though I had a sneaking suspicion this wasn't her first time. I wondered – just for a second – if perhaps Paris was attracted to Mark's folksy and laid back attitude. If she was, I couldn't blame her. Her boyfriend was ugly. What? I said I was shallow.

Still, Paris didn't overtly flirt with Mark. For his part, Mark split his time between watching Paris navigate the treacherous sidewalk and trying to engage me in conversation. Luckily for me, the conversation was of the mundane variety.

Which bands did I like? Band of Horses ruled.

What was my favorite movie? *The Goonies* still stands up today.

What was my favorite book? *Lord of the Rings* was cool before the movies. It's still cool after.

Did I like comic books? No, but I did like super hero movies.

We had a lot in common. I couldn't help but smile at him. He was a nice guy. And, after my run-ins with Aric and Rafael over the past two days, it was nice to find a guy I just wanted to hang out with and not picture naked.

Whew, I wasn't in heat after all.

After Paris had monopolized the skateboard for a full hour, she brought it over to me. I looked at it dubiously. It had seemed like a good idea in the cafeteria. That really wasn't the case anymore. Still, I didn't want to look like a wimp.

Here's the thing, skateboards and in-line skates clearly aren't my thing. I have no sense of balance. I wasn't on the skateboard five seconds before I crashed to the ground and skinned my elbow.

Both Mark and Paris tried to cajole me back onto the death contraption, but I declined – with profanity. After ten minutes, they both gave up and we agreed to walk over to the 7-Eleven for a Slurpee before returning to the dorms.

While we were sitting at a picnic table outside the convenience store drinking our Slurpees and enjoying the nice weather – and the beginnings of what looked like a terrific sunset – my cellphone vibrated in my pocket.

I reached for it and saw that it was Will calling. We'd both agreed to wait until Monday to talk. I guess he missed me. I smiled a little bit at the thought. This was going to work out great.

"Hey," I greeted him.

"Hey, how's it going?" Will was kind of a slacker at first glance. That was only the surface, though. He worked to put himself through school. His parents were moronic hippies who spent more time at Renaissance fairs than raising him and his brother. They even built a teepee in their backyard to live in during the summer. I'm not joking. It was baffling. I think they just did it so they could smoke their peace pipe near nature and not share it with their kids, although I had no proof of that.

"It's going good."

"You get your books?"

"Yeah."

"You get all your stuff unpacked?"

"Yeah."

"You know where all the buildings you have to go to tomorrow are?"

"Yes, Dad," I sighed in irritation. I could tell Will was smiling on the other side of the phone.

"You're all set then, right? You've done everything you have to do?"

"I said yes."

"Good, you want to come over and do me?"

Wow, I stepped right into that one. "Do I want to come over and do you?"

"He's a smooth talker," Paris giggled.

I noticed Mark's eyes had darkened slightly. He was clearly listening to the conversation – even though he was pretending not to.

"Why don't you come over here?"

Will snorted.

"What was that noise?"

"I'm not coming to the dorms."

"Why not?"

"I'm a junior."

"So?"

"So, juniors aren't seen at the freshman dorms. People will talk."

"People will talk about what?"

"They'll say I'm trying to pick up a freshman or something."

"You are trying to pick up a freshman."

"No, I've already picked up a freshman – a hot freshman." Well, that placated me a little bit. "A hot freshman who I've known for years and been having sex with for a respectable amount of time."

I was getting annoyed again. "What's your point?"

"I'm not coming to the dorms."

"Well, I'm not walking to your frat house."

"I'll come pick you up."

"So you'll come pick me up at the dorms, but you won't come into the dorms?"

"Right."

"That's ridiculous."

"It is what it is."

"I guess you're sleeping alone tonight then, Mr. Junior."

Will paused on the other end of the phone. I could tell he was mulling things over. This hadn't worked how he thought it would. He decided to try a different tact.

"I wanted you to meet my frat brothers."

"I met them when you moved in two weeks ago."

"Not all of them."

"I met enough of them. You haven't met my roommates."

"I'll do that later."

"When?"

"Later."

Now I was really getting irritated. "Just come over here."

Will decided to dig his heels in. "I don't want to go over there."

"Well, I'm staying here tonight." I realized we'd both started yelling at one another somewhere in the last few minutes. I struggled to bring my tone down. People were starting to stare.

"Fine," Will was clearly as aggravated as I felt.

"Fine," I agreed.

There was an uncomfortable silence. Will finally broke it. "I'll come over and meet your roommates tomorrow."

"Thank you."

After disconnecting, I couldn't help but wonder if this wasn't going to be as great of an arrangement as I had originally thought.

6 SIX

The first day of classes came quick – seemingly too quick, for a slacker like me, anyway.

Technically, I'm not a slacker. I am academically lazy, though. Things have just always come easy for me when it comes to school (math notwithstanding). I have a borderline photographic memory – which has been a godsend when it comes to schoolwork. Also, I can write faster than most people can read – so that's also been a benefit. The problem is, the ease in which I've approached school has made me indifferent when it comes to pursuing higher education.

College was going to be different, I promised myself. I was not only going to embrace an academic environment, I was going to pursue it.

I'm not sure I totally believe it either – but it is a righteous goal.

My first class didn't start until 10 a.m., so Paris and I both got up early and got ready. Brittany's first class had been at 8 a.m. She'd actually been excited about it. I thought that all classes should have been offered after noon. I didn't get to decide these things, though.

I wasn't sure what time Tara's first class was, but she was gone before Paris and I even got out of bed. Since we still had half an hour before we had to leave, we decided to stuff ourselves with a quick breakfast. I doubted that would be a normal thing – but I figured we might as well take advantage of being up while we could.

After eating some eggs and hash-browns – I noted with disgust that Paris drowned her breakfast in ketchup – we headed off for our first day of academic success.

"Are you nervous?"

Paris and I were going to the same building – even if we didn't have a class together until later in the afternoon. She was starting off her day with English 101 just like I was – she just had a different professor. After that we had astronomy together and then I finished the day with Journalism 101.

"No, are you nervous?" I actually wasn't nervous. I think it was fair to say I was cautiously optimistic.

"Not really. I just don't know what to expect."

"Me either," I admitted. "In high school it was easy. I don't think this is going to be as easy."

"I don't think you'll have too much trouble," she said.

"I hope not."

We walked in companionable silence for a few minutes. I could tell something was on her mind. "How's Mike?"

"He's fine."

"How's Will?"

He's an asshole. "He's fine."

We lapsed into silence again.

"Aren't you glad we both have boyfriends so we don't have to go through this whole mating ritual of looking for someone, like Brittany?"

"Totally."

"Totally," Paris echoed.

I wondered if my reply sounded as hollow as hers did.

"Aric seemed nice." I thought that was a little pointed.

"I don't know about nice."

"He seemed hot."

"He's definitely hot."

Paris giggled and I couldn't help but join in. "I just don't think he's nice."

"You don't know him."

"No," I conceded.

"Do you want to know him?"

"No!" I felt like I'd answered that a little too quickly. Maybe she hadn't noticed.

"I'd want to know him."

"You seem like you want to know Mark." There it was. I'd said it out loud.

"What do you mean?"

"I mean you seem interested in Mark."

"He's nice. He's just fun to hang out with." Paris was getting defensive.

"Fine."

"Fine."

"He's cute, though."

"He's totally cute," she agreed.

The Covenant College campus isn't big – which is a plus. It's not tiny like a community college or anything, but it's not so big that you can't walk to class either.

The building Paris and I were going to was located close to our dorm and nearly adjacent to the UC. Luckily for me, the bulk of my classes were located in this building. Since I was a journalism major – or at least thought I would stay one – most of my classes would remain in this building. Once Paris started getting into the core of her curriculum, though, she would have to walk to a building on the far edge of campus.

Once we got into Leeland Hall, we both found ourselves checking our class schedules. My class was on the second floor and hers was on the first. We said our goodbyes at the stairwell.

"See you in an hour for astronomy," she said brightly.

I smiled and waved to her as I climbed up the flight of stairs.

When I got to class, I was surprised it was so small. It was certainly bigger than my high school classes had been – but it was also small enough to be considered cozy.

The rest of the class filed in before the professor – a dazed looking woman who declared all modern literature dead – made her first appearance. Even though I found the teacher scattered, the class looked easy. I only had to read five books for the semester and write five papers. That wouldn't be hard at all.

After class, I traipsed back down to a lecture hall for my astronomy class. Paris had gotten there first and saved me a seat. This was what I always pictured college to be like -- a big auditorium with hundreds of kids milling about and forming cliques. I was actually surprised that so many kids wanted to take astronomy – but then again they were probably like Paris and me. They just didn't want to dissect anything.

The class went by pretty quickly. The actual lecture didn't seem like it was going to be hard. The lab portion, though, was probably going to be a pain. We were going to have to go up on top of the science building – no matter how cold it was – to draw star maps. Paris didn't seem deterred – but she was an art major. That didn't sound fun to me at all.

After class, I bid Paris goodbye and walked to the far end of the building where my Journalism 101 class was going to be held.

When I entered I was relieved to find myself in another small class environment.

The class was pretty full, but I slid into a desk next to a pretty girl who looked like she had some Italian heritage to go along with her darker skin and full mane of wavy brown hair. I smiled at her as I sat.

"I'm Matilda," she said immediately. I was glad to see that she didn't try to shake my hand.

"Zoe," I replied.

"Is journalism your major?"

I considered her question seriously. "It is right now."

"Yeah, I'm not all that sure either," she said.

Matilda and I exchanged mindless chatter for a few minutes. I found out she lived one floor above me in the dorms – oh, and she was obsessed with one of the Ricks. I wasn't sure which one, but if I had to guess I figured it was the hot one, aka Rick No. 1.

"Do you know him?"

"We've met."

"Do you like him?"

"He seems fine. I haven't had a chance to talk to him all that much."

"Well, now I have a reason to be down on your floor."

I must have looked confused.

"We have class together. We can study together."

I'd always considered studying to be a solo endeavor, but I let it slide. I figured this was just some mindless infatuation that she'd get over – or maybe I just hoped.

I noticed the class had gone silent and I turned my attention to the front of the room. I wasn't sure what I expected, but this wasn't it. The guy who had taken his place up at the podium looked young – not student young -- but like forty-young. Instead of a suit – like I'd seen other professors in the hallway clad in – he was wearing blue jeans and a rock T-shirt. Sure, it was a Strokes T-shirt, but he could have been wearing a Nickelback shirt or something and really thrown my day off.

"I'm Sam Blake," he introduced himself, flashing his bright blue eyes around the room. I couldn't help but think he was awfully hot for a professor. "You can call me Sam or Mr. Blake. You can also call me professor, but I sometimes forget I'm a professor, so I might not answer you."

I heard a few giggles behind me and turned to see a group of four girls flashing him big smiles. What a bunch of whores. *Whoa, where did that come from?*

Sam continued to prove that he wasn't a normal teacher. Instead of pulling out a syllabus, he went around the room and had all of us stand up to introduce ourselves.

When it got to be my turn, I was a little nervous but I didn't see any harm in the endeavor. "I'm Zoe."

"What's your last name Zoe?"

"Lake."

"Where are you from Zoe?"

"Uh, a small town about an hour away from Traverse City."

Sam Blake's eyes narrowed slightly as he looked at me. "What town is that?"

"Why does it matter?" I challenged. I don't know why it was such a big deal, but I wasn't keen on divulging my hometown.

"I guess it doesn't," Sam said. "I was just curious why it was such a secret?"

"I didn't say it was a secret."

"So which town is it?"

"Barker Creek."

Sam raised his eyebrows in surprise. "See, was that so hard?"

I fought to hide my distaste from him.

"That's a pretty area."

That surprised me. Most people had never even heard of Barker Creek, let alone been there.

"It's okay."

"Good skiing."

Well, that made more sense. He had been to the nearby resort. "Yes."

"Do you ski?" Now I was on edge. He hadn't asked anyone else this many questions.

"Yes."

"You golf?"

"No." The resort was a golf course in the summer.

"There's a lot of legend that surrounds that area."

Now I was really confused. "What legend?"

"Just legends."

"What legends? You mean the Dog Man?"

Sam actually smiled to himself this time. "Yes, the Dog Man."

"What's the Dog Man?" I wasn't sure who asked the question, but it was someone sitting behind me.

"It's nothing," I muttered.

"No, Zoe, tell the class about the Dog Man. It might make a good lesson."

"The Dog Man is Bigfoot." My answer was terse, so terse that Sam gave me a pointed frown.

"Bigfoot? That's ridiculous." Another voice from the crowd.

Sam was still giving me 'the look.' I sighed resignedly. "It's not really Bigfoot. I mean it is, but it's not. There are all these stories up there about seven-foot-tall-dog-men attacking people."

I turned and looked and saw that half the class was trying to hide their smirks and the other half seemed mesmerized.

"Weren't most of the attacks around the turn of the century?" Sam again.

"Actually, the legend has it that there's an attack every seven years." I noticed that Sam seemed to nod ever-so-slightly when I gave my answer.

I was starting to feel uncomfortable. "It's just a legend they tell to mess with tourists. They even have a song up there that they play called *The Legend* that's about the Dog Man. I have it on my iPod," I offered lamely.

I could hear a few snickers now.

"Have you ever seen a Dog Man?" Matilda had been one of the students enthralled with the conversation. She had asked the question with absolutely no guile.

"No."

"That's too bad."

Sam was looking at me funny. It was almost like he was going to challenge me. He must have decided better.

"So, class, how does this tie into journalism?"

I was relieved to be able to take my seat and listen to the class expound on the virtues of oral legend vs. gossip -- but something about Sam Blake wasn't sitting right with me.

"This whole place is weird," I muttered under my breath.

"What did you say?" Matilda was looking at me quizzically.

"Nothing."

As I met Sam Blake's cool blue gaze again, I had a weird feeling that nothing was going to turn into something – and soon.

7 SEVEN

I wanted to leave class quickly – mostly because Sam Blake's insistent questioning unnerved me. Matilda wasn't about to let that happen, though. She wouldn't stop her inane chatter and the next thing I knew we were walking out of the class together. At least Sam hadn't tried to talk to me again, although I did notice him watching me leave.

Matilda not only walked all the way back to the dorms with me, but she walked all the way to my room with me. I think she was hoping for a glimpse of Rick No. 1. Luckily, his dorm room was closed.

It took me about fifteen minutes to get her to leave – even though I was dropping anvils about being tired. When she finally did, I was relieved.

Paris walked in about five minutes after she left. "How was your journalism class?"

Weird. "Fine."

"You want dinner?"

"Yeah," I hastily looked down at my Fossil watch. "Will is going to be here in two hours, so let's go get dinner now."

Paris and I made our way to the cafeteria – where we both noticed that Tara and Brittany were already seated with some other people from our floor. I noticed both Ricks were there and smiled to myself. I had told Paris about Matilda's Rick fascination and she laughed when she saw him, too.

"How much you want to bet she starts eating with us?"

I looked around the cafeteria stealthily. I didn't see her. For now we were safe.

Dinner that night included chicken and a baked potato bar. When we joined the others, Brittany was in the middle of recounting her day.

"I had four classes and I think I'm going to learn a lot from all of them."

Paris and I exchanged small smiles.

Brittany turned to us. "How were your classes?"

"Fine."

Brittany pursed her lips.

"I think we're going to learn a lot, too," I said in a superficially high voice. Sarcasm was apparently lost on her.

"Good. I think you'll do better with some structure."

Where had that come from?

Rick No. 1, the hot one, turned to me. "Are you basking in the knowledge?"

I snorted. "Oh, yeah, I'm just soaking it all in."

Everyone chatted easily for the next hour before we all returned to our rooms. I watched Brittany immediately go to her desk in the bedroom, pull out her textbooks and a pink highlighter, and diligently start reading.

I threw myself in the wicker chair and turned on the television. Will would be here relatively soon.

Paris sat down on the futon couch and watched television with me. We settled on an episode of Hoarders.

"I love this show," she said.

"Me, too. These people are such freaks."

"I feel sorry for them," Tara chimed in, sitting on the couch next to Paris.

I saw Brittany give us all dirty looks from the bedroom, but opted to ignore her. If we were being too loud there were study rooms at the end of the hall.

About halfway through the episode, there was a knock at the door. We had left it open, but Will had stopped at the threshold and knocked out of respect. He was good that way.

When I saw him, I realized I honestly had missed him. It had been almost five days since we'd seen each other. He was dressed in a simple pair of jeans and faded T-shirt, but his brown eyes were accented nicely by his summer tan.

"Hey," I got up and gave him a warm hug.

Will had looked apprehensive at first. I think he was worried I was still going to be mad about yesterday.

Paris gave him a welcoming smile as I disengaged myself and introduced him to everyone.

I saw Brittany get up from the desk and come out to greet him. "You must be the famous Will."

Will slid me a sly look, pushing his dusky hair behind his ears. "I'm famous, huh?"

"Only in your own mind," I teased.

Despite his reservations about coming to the dorms, Will sat down in the wicker chair and pulled me on his lap as he conversed with my roommates. I realized that he had missed me, too.

After about a half an hour of conversation, I turned to him. "Now what?"

"What do you mean?"

"Are we going back to your house?"

He seemed surprised. "I didn't think that was an option."

"Well, you've been a good boy, I guess you deserve a reward."

Will smirked. "You mean you got your way and now you're willing to compromise."

"That's an ugly thing to say."

"I've known you for four years. I know the way your mind works."

I smiled at him. The truth was, I had really missed him – and we couldn't do the things I was thinking about in a dorm room which three other girls slept in.

"Go pack an overnight bag," he whispered, brushing his lips against my ear as he pushed me up.

It only took me a few minutes to get my things together. When I walked back into the common room, Brittany was frowning.

"What?" I was quickly losing my patience with her.

"What about classes tomorrow?"

"What about them?"

"Aren't you going to go?"

"Yeah, I'll just walk from Will's house."

Brittany still looked unhappy.

"What's your deal?"

I saw her cut Will a suspicious look and then grab my arm and drag me back into the bedroom. "Are you going to have sex with him?"

Oh, this ought to be good. "Why do you ask that?"

"You're spending the night with him."

"So? It's not the first time."

"Your parents let you have sex with him?"

"They weren't there, so I don't think they knew about it."

"What if you get pregnant?"

"That's what birth control is for."

"You're on birth control?" Brittany practically yelled the question. I saw Will smirk through the door and shake his head slightly.

"Yeah, I've been on it for years."

"Why?"

"Because I don't want to have a baby."

Brittany looked nonplussed.

"Well, you better be careful," she said finally.

"Thanks, Mom."

Will and I left. I was proud of him. He waited until we got on the elevator before he dissolved into laughter. "She's a trip."

"She's a pain."

Will eyed me sagely. "You just aren't used to living with other people. You're an only child. You're spoiled."

"I'm not spoiled."

"Please, you're the most spoiled person I know and I'm partially to blame for it."

"Why do you say that?"

"Who is the one who compromised? That's right, me. I always compromise and then you compromise. I have to compromise first, though."

"You shouldn't think of it as compromising," I said lightly. "You should think of it as doing the right thing."

"Because you're always right?"

"Not always."

"When aren't you right?"

"Remember when I told you that 98 Degrees were rock gods when I was fourteen?"

Will smirked.

"I couldn't have been more wrong about that."

Will laced his fingers through mine as we left the building, pulling me close. I really had missed him.

It took us about ten minutes to drive to the other side of campus and park at his dorm. He led me into the house and I was surprised to see a group of about twenty guys gathered in the living room watching a handful of frat brothers play Garage Band.

"Working hard, I see."

"It's the first day," Will said. "Nothing happens on the first day."

"You didn't want to play Garage Band?"

Will smiled at me seductively. "I guess you could say I wanted to play with you more."

Yep, it was going to be a good night.

"Do me a favor, though," he seemed slightly nervous. "Go in

there with me and be nice to them for five minutes before we go downstairs."

"Did you think I would be mean?"

"Like I said, I know you. Please don't be mean."

I let Will lead me into the living room. He introduced me to the guys – some of whom I'd already met – but none of them seemed overly excited to see me.

I let my attention drift to the television screen and couldn't help but laugh. They were horrible at this game. I didn't say that out loud, though.

Will was over talking to one of his brothers and I kind of pushed myself out of the way to wait. The room felt like one big burst of testosterone. I guess that's what happens when you put a bunch of guys in a house together, give them beer and then let them play with phallic instruments.

Despite the ease that the guys were expressing with each other I couldn't help but feel that someone was watching me. I turned to look at Will, but he was still talking to his frat brother. I had that distinctive prick in the middle of my back, though, and I knew that meant that someone was watching me.

I tried to discreetly scan the room. None of the guys focused on the game had even noticed me, though. I turned and focused on a figure standing in the corner – an extremely big figure – that was positioned behind everyone else. It was Aric – the behemoth from the UC. He was leaning against the wall with his broad arms crossed over his expansive chest. He was staring at me.

For a second, it was like all the oxygen had been sucked out of the room and there weren't twenty other guys standing there shouting at a video game. It was like the two of us were stuck in a vacuum.

Then, just as suddenly as the feeling had washed over me, it was gone and I felt a presence slide in behind me. It was Will.

"Ready to go downstairs?"

I turned to him, plastering a smile on my face to hide my discomfort. "Absolutely. I've had my fill of Aerosmith."

"Hey, some of their earlier stuff was good."

I laughed hollowly, shooting a look back at Aric. He was still staring at me. I noticed Will look at Aric, too. He frowned when he saw him staring. I expected him to say something, even joke about his weird fraternity brother; instead he pretended he hadn't noticed.

I took Will's hand and followed him toward the steps. I turned back briefly, but Aric was no longer leaning against the wall. I wasn't sure where he went, but he'd definitely left me unnerved.

8 EIGHT

The next morning I woke up slightly disoriented – and tired. My sleep pattern the night before had been fitful, and I'd been plagued by bloody dreams – but for the life of me I couldn't remember them. I could only remember a wall of red – and what distinctly sounded like howls of pain.

I rolled over to find that Will was still asleep next to me. I marveled for a moment at how serene he looked in sleep before I climbed out of bed to get ready for class.

Despite fraternity horror stories, Will had his own bathroom in the basement apartment so I left him to sleep while I showered. After braiding my hair to keep it out of my face for the day and getting dressed, I walked back out into Will's bedroom.

"Morning," he murmured.

"Morning."

"What time is your first class?"

"Not until 11 a.m."

"You want breakfast?"

"Where?"

"Here."

"Nah. I don't really want to hang out with your frat brothers," I said it matter-of-factly, but I thought maybe I was a little too harsh when I saw the look on Will's face. "I mean, you know how crabby I am in the morning." It was a lame excuse, but it was all I had.

Will didn't respond, but I could tell he wasn't happy with my declaration.

"I'll just grab something at the UC really quick." God, I hope he's not going to pout.

"Do you want me to drive you to class?" I figured he couldn't be that mad if he was offering to be helpful. I didn't want to push him, though.

"No, I'm fine. It's only a fifteen-minute walk. I could use the exercise."

Will smiled for the first time that morning as he pulled me to his lap. "I thought you got plenty of exercise last night."

When Will tries to be sexy, sometimes it comes off as creepy. "Well, since I did all the work," I teased. One look at Will's face told me now was not the time to go there. I kissed the tip of his nose to placate him instead. "What's your day like?"

When in doubt, divert. That's one of my golden rules.

"Nothing really. I have one class and then a lab this afternoon. What about you?"

"Just two classes."

"You want to come back over tonight?"

"I should probably wait and see if I get any homework." I didn't mention that. I didn't want to sleep in the dark basement room again. There was something about it that was giving me the creeps.

"Since when do you do homework?"

"Well, it hasn't happened yet, but I'm trying to develop a new work ethic."

Will barked out a laugh, which he quickly bit back when I shot an angry look at him. "That's a good idea."

"You're a horrible liar."

Will watched me pack my book bag quietly for a few moments before speaking again. "Your roommates seem nice."

I raised my eyebrow at him questioningly.

"Okay, Paris seems nice. I think you'll get along fine with her. Brittany is a little weird."

"Brittany is wound a little tight."

"You need to loosen her up," Will agreed.

"I'm afraid if we do that then she's going to go crazy."

"What do you mean?" Will climbed out of bed and slipped into a pair of boxer shorts. I admired his muscular rear end for a few minutes – wistfully wishing we had enough time for a quickie – before returning my attention to my book bag. I could tell by Will's sly smirk he'd seen me checking him out.

"I mean that she needs to get laid."

"That's for sure. What's wrong with that?"

"Nothing is wrong with it. She just has one of those personalities where when she finally does get laid she's going to go crazy and sleep with everything that moves for six months – and that's going to be a whole other set of problems."

Will quirked a suggestive smile in my direction. "Is that what happened to you?"

Now it was my turn to let loose with a shrill laugh. "I was sixteen when I first had sex. Trust me, you were all I could handle. She's treating her virginity like some prize, though. Nothing good ever happens when you make such a big deal about it."

Will was quiet for a second.

"What?"

"I was just thinking about how hard it must be to be a girl some-times." I couldn't help but smile at how serious his dark eyes were.

"Yeah, well, it's easier than being a boy sometimes."

"How do you figure?"

I figured that was a loaded question, so I decided to skirt it.

"You want to walk me up?"

"You're not going to answer my question?"

"I'll be late."

I could tell Will was debating pushing me on the issue. Instead he merely shrugged and pulled himself up from the bed.

We climbed the stairs to the main floor quietly. I wasn't sure how many of his frat brothers would be up – but I most certainly didn't want to see Aric. Something was weird about that whole situation.

When we made it up to the main floor I took a look around the living room. It was littered with empty beer bottles and pizza boxes.

"Well, for one thing, girls are cleaner than boys."

"Huh?"

"Why it's harder to be a boy. You have to live in filth."

Will smirked. He leaned in to give me a kiss goodbye. "Call me later."

I nodded and let myself out the front door. I noticed Will making his way back downstairs. I figured he was probably going to get another couple of hours of sleep.

As I happily skipped down the steps, I caught a flurry of movement coming up the driveway. I opened my mouth to say hi when I realized it was Aric. I snapped my mouth shut. I was hoping I'd be able to make my getaway without him saying anything. No such luck.

"Did you spend the night here?" Aric looked irritated. I found that fairly interesting – and by interesting I mean creepy.

"Why do you care?"

"It was just a question."

"Yes, I spent the night."

"You're dating Will." It wasn't a question, but I answered anyway.

"Yes, I'm dating Will."

"Where did you meet?"

"When I was fourteen he came to my school dance."

"What?" Aric looked confused.

"We know each other from home." Sometimes you have to make things simplistic for men.

"So you've known him a long time?"

"Four years."

"Have you dated him all four years?"

"What is this, twenty questions?" Aric's busybody nature was starting to irk me.

"Are you embarrassed by your relationship?"

"No."

"Then why not just answer?"

"I will when you tell me why you care."

"He's a friend. I've just never heard of you."

My eyes narrowed as I regarded Aric. I could tell he wanted me to react to that statement. While it hurt, I wasn't going to let him know it hurt.

"Maybe you're not as close of friends as you thought you were?"

"Maybe. Or maybe you're not as important to him as you think you are?"

Well, that was low.

"Thanks for the morale booster. If you'll excuse me?" I tried to push past the wall of muscle that was Aric. He didn't budge.

I blew out a frustrated sigh. "What is your deal?"

"What makes you think I have a deal?"

"The fact that I've now met you twice and you've invaded my personal space both times."

"Maybe I think you're hot."

"There are plenty of hot girls here." God, I hoped my face wasn't flaming red.

Aric grudgingly took a step back to let me pass. "I'm sorry."

At first I wasn't sure he had said anything at all. I paused as I was moving past him and looked up into his eyes searchingly for a second. "What are you sorry about?"

"I shouldn't have said what I did to you about Will."

"It doesn't matter."

"Why not?"

"Because my relationship isn't contingent on you. I know that's mind boggling."

Aric smiled at me – a true smile – one that reached all the way up to his chocolate eyes. I couldn't help but notice how much more attractive he was when he smiled.

"You think I'm conceited."

"I think you're used to women falling at your feet."

"But not you?"

"No, not me."

I decided now was the time to make my escape and continued down the driveway. I wanted to look back to see if he was still there, but I realized I'd look much cooler if I didn't. It was hard, but I managed to make the trek out to the road.

I started toward the campus, all the while fighting the inner urge to look back. As I made it to the end of the street and started to turn, I risked a quick glance back. Not only was Aric still there, but also he was still staring.

I felt a little pride that he was still checking me out – at first. Then I realized that I had only met him twice and I'd been rude both times.

A wave of creepiness began to wash over me again. I made a mental note to find a way to grill Will about Aric, without making it obvious what I was after. A guy who chased a girl who was not only dating his friend but treated him like dirt might have some sort of personality disorder, after all.

Without realizing what I was doing, I raised a hand to wave at Aric as I drifted out of sight. Well, so much for being cool.

9 NINE

Classes that day were not only uneventful, they were ridiculously boring. I was actually relieved. Within the last three days I'd met three different men who had managed to unnerve me – and one of them was an extremely strange professor.

After my second class of the day, I happily trudged back to the dorms alone. When I made it up to the room, Brittany and Tara were in the bedroom studiously toiling away at their desks. Paris was sitting on the couch watching General Hospital. I joined her.

"How was your night?"

"Fine." I wanted to talk to Paris about Aric, but I didn't know how to broach the subject. How do you explain a feeling?

"You do anything fun?"

"Just each other."

Paris smirked as I levied my attention on General Hospital. We silently watched the soap for a few minutes before I turned back to her. "You spend the night at Mike's last night?"

"Yeah."

"You going back tonight?"

"No." I noticed she grimaced.

"What's wrong?"

"It's nothing."

"Tell me."

Paris sighed – one of those long ones that only come when you've been dating the same guy for a long time and you've had to suffer through a lot of bullshit. "He gave himself a nickname."

"What do you mean?"

"I mean, he gave himself a nickname and he wants everyone to start calling him it."

"What is it?"

"Boots."

"Boots?"

"Boots."

"That's a stupid nickname. Why did he give himself that name?"

"Because he wants everyone to know that he's constantly knocking boots."

My mouth must have dropped open in surprise because the next thing I knew I was forcing it shut. "You're shitting me."

"Nope."

"What is it with guys?"

"I know, right?"

We both turned our attention back to the television. After the show ended, everyone decided to have an early dinner. Tara and Brittany had 'loads' of homework to fill their night.

"Do you have anything?" Paris asked curiously as we walked down the hallway.

"Nope."

"Me either."

We ended up eating dinner with the guys across the hall. They were excited because they'd seen one of the girls down the hall – Natalie, I think her name was -- naked. Apparently she'd walked across the common room nude because she didn't realize the door between the hall and the room was open.

"How did she look?" Brittany was appalled at my question.

"What do you mean?" Rick No. 2 asked.

"Does she stuff?"

"How should I know?"

"Her boobs always look lumpy. I assumed she stuffed."

The conversation didn't progress from that point. Everyone started debating whether or not Natalie stuffed. I couldn't wait until our conjecture made its way down the hall to her. She was already a bitch. I figured this would push her over the edge -- to raving bitch.

After dinner, Paris and I both lamented our lack of anything to do.

"You could go back over to Will's," she offered.

I turned to her conspiratorially. "His room is in the basement."

"So."

"So, there's no window and it kind of creeps me out. It's like being in a box -- or an animal den -- or something. It's freaky."

"Don't tell him that."

"I know. He's so fricking sensitive."

"He's a man. They say we're the only ones who get PMS – but they are definitely mistaken."

We ultimately decided to go down to Mark's floor and get him. "I could use a Slurpee," I agreed.

Mark was eager to join us. I noticed he left the skateboard behind this time and purposely positioned himself between us as we made the walk to the 7-Eleven.

We chatted amiably about classes, home, the weather – anything that wouldn't be considered heavy. After getting our Slurpees, we sat at the picnic table outside the 7-Eleven and continued to chat. Finally, Mark broke our unspoken rule and asked a question neither Paris nor I wanted to answer.

"So you both have serious boyfriends, huh?"

"I don't know if you'd call them serious," Paris answered. I had a sneaking suspicion that Boots' days were numbered.

"Will and I are kind of serious," I offered. I couldn't help but notice that Mark seemed a little bit disappointed.

"How long have you been together?"

"Four years."

Mark looked nonplussed. Four years was a lot of history to overcome. Of course, he didn't know that we frequently took "time outs" during those four years – and I had no intention of telling him. As nice as he was, Mark just wasn't my cup of tea on a romantic level.

After that, the conversation veered back into a safe area and I could see that both Paris and I had visibly relaxed.

As we walked back to the dorms, I noticed that it looked like it was about to start raining.

"I hope it storms."

"You like storms?"

"Yeah."

"Me, too," Paris admitted.

"Me three," Mark chimed in.

We decided to wait outside to see if it would storm. We weren't disappointed. Paris and I both walked out into the open field next to the dorm, opening our arms and staring up at the sky as the downpour started.

"I love the rain," Paris said.

I was only half listening to her. The truth is, I felt relaxed during a storm. Other people got keyed up and scared. I was just the opposite. I was one of those rare people who felt no harm could ever come to me in a storm. The rest of the time, of course, was another story.

Without even speaking to each other, Paris and I both began twirling in the storm. There was no rhyme or reason behind our movements, we both just wanted to be free.

For his part, Mark was quickly getting bored.

"Let's go inside."

There was a loud crack of thunder. Neither Paris nor I were dissuaded from the twirling.

Mark was starting to get panicky. "Seriously, let's go inside before we get struck by lightning."

Paris and I ignored Mark's plea.

The next thing I knew, something cold and wet splattered against the left side of my head. I reached up to feel what it was. I realized it was mud. I turned in the direction it had come from.

Rick No. 1 was doubled over laughing a few feet away. The rest of his suite mates were next to him.

Now, a normal girl would have been agitated by mud being thrown at her. I was exhilarated. Before I even realized what was happening I'd retaliated with such force that Rick No. 1 had actually slipped and fallen in the mud in his haste to get away.

These movements set off a full-on mud fight amongst everyone.

The fight was a melee of bodies and molded dirt that lasted a full half an hour before everyone had their fill. We made our way into the dorm and all climbed into the elevator together. Everyone was still laughing and having a good time as they made their way down the hall. I noticed our dorm room was open – which surprised me. I thought Tara and Brittany were hard at work on their homework.

When I entered the door, I realized that it hadn't been left open by my roommates. Instead, Will was sitting on the couch expectantly.

When he saw me, drenched and covered with mud, his brow furrowed.

"What happened?"

"Nothing," I laughed. "We just had a mud fight."

Will glared at the guys standing behind us in the hall. They seemed to get the hint and quickly exited to their own room. Mark whispered a quick goodbye and took off for the stairwell at the end of the hall.

"What's wrong?" I didn't understand why Will was so worked up. We didn't have any plans. I was sure of it.

"What do you mean what's wrong? You're covered in mud."

"So?"

"You're covered in mud and wet."

"If you're worried about the mess, it's not like I'm making a mess at your place."

"It's not the mess!" Will practically exploded.

"Then what is it?" I was no happier with him than he was with me right now.

"It's ... it's ... ."

"What?"

"It's just so childish."

"Childish? It's childish?"

Will nodded mutely.

"You had black eyes all summer because you threw lit firecrackers in your brother's room when he was trying to get it on with a girl and he beat the crap out of you and I'm childish?"

"That's different." Will looked uncomfortable.

"How is that different?"

"Because that was at home."

"So?"

"That was at home – where my brothers couldn't find out about it."

"Why would your frat brothers care that I got in a mud fight?"

Will shifted uncomfortably. I got the feeling he'd said something he wished he could take back. Quite frankly, I wished he could take the whole visit back.

"I guess they wouldn't."

"Then why are you so upset?"

"I guess I just didn't like seeing you flirt with those guys." Will averted his eyes from me. The statement had a ring of truth – and yet I didn't think it was the truth.

Given the fact that I was wet and dripping on the floor, though, I didn't have the energy to fight with Will.

"Well then," I said in a measured and clipped tone. "I guess you just shouldn't tell your frat brothers I was in a mud fight and you should realize that engaging in a mud fight isn't equitable to sex."

Will nodded, still uncomfortable with the situation.

Things didn't get much better after that. Will made a hasty retreat – promising to call me tomorrow – and Brittany gave Paris and

I dirty looks until we'd cleaned the floor in the common area to her approval.

After everything was done, Paris and I both climbed on the couch and flipped channels until we found an episode of *Hoarders* to watch.

"Still totally worth it," Paris whispered.

10 TEN

Most people say that if you sleep on it, most of your anger will abate during the night.

The people that say that are wrong.

When I woke up the next morning I was still angry with Will. I was also suspicious. I couldn't figure out why he would possibly care what we'd done the night before.

Since it was Wednesday, I had the same class schedule as Monday. I wasn't looking forward to returning to Journalism 101 and the peculiar Mr. Blake – speaking of things that were making me suspicious. That was getting to be a long list.

Paris and I went to breakfast together. Neither of us seemed up for much conversation, though. I figured she was struggling with her feelings for Mike. I knew I was struggling with how to make my relationship with Will work – especially after his juvenile shit fit the night before.

After eating a huge plate of cheesy hash-browns, Paris and I set out for class. Any conversation we did share was light.

We split up to head to different floors. English was uneventful –

as usual. Paris and I met back up for Astronomy – which was ridiculously boring.

"I thought this was going to be more fun," Paris admitted.

"Me, too."

"That lab is going to suck."

"No doubt."

After Astronomy, I slowly made my way toward the Journalism
101 class. I stopped to tie my shoes – even though they didn't need it
– and get a drink of water, even though I wasn't thirsty. I was just
dreading seeing Professor Blake again.

When I entered the classroom, I tried to ignore Matilda waving at
me frantically.

"Zoe! I saved you a seat."

I guess I couldn't ignore that. I grimaced as I slid into the seat
next to Matilda and greeted her with as much enthusiasm as I could
muster – which admittedly wasn't much.

"I was worried you weren't coming."

"Why?"

"I don't know. You were almost late."

I decided to try to ignore her for the rest of the class. That wasn't
in the cards either.

"So, has Rick said anything about me?"

"Which Rick?"

"The good-looking one."

"Ah, Rick No. 1," I shoved a piece of gum in my mouth and
feigned like I was thinking hard. "No, I don't think so."

One look at Matilda's crestfallen face and I actually wished I
had lied.

"I don't see him that often, though," I offered.

"Why not?"

Because I don't stalk him like you do. "Because we have classes.
And I have a boyfriend."

"Oh, you have a boyfriend?" Matilda was looking way too interested in that little tidbit. *Crap.*

"Yeah."

"He's here?"

I sighed as I explained about Will. I told her the bare minimum of information. I couldn't take much more of this.

Luckily for me – or maybe unluckily – Professor Blake decided to make his appearance at this point. I was relieved when he didn't even glance my way. Maybe I had imagined everything.

Mr. Blake greeted the class and then sat on the edge of his desk.

"A lot of journalism is about perception," he said.

I noticed everyone was busily typing on their laptops and iPads so I dutifully pulled my iPad out – even though I didn't think Professor Blake had said anything profound yet.

"This isn't the same news era that your parents grew up in and it's especially not the same era of news reporting that your grandparents grew up in," he continued.

"What do you mean?" One of the students in the back row – a girl – was trying to act like she was studiously involved in the lecture for Professor Blake's benefit.

"I mean, when your parents and grandparents were younger, the news business was different. News has changed – and I think the biggest change is that a lot of people look at news for its entertainment value," he said.

"Can you be more specific?" The same girl. She was going to be annoying.

"News broadcasts used to be just about the news. A straight-up rundown of the facts," he said. "Now, though, you have personalities that slant the news – and it's not just one news organization. You have news being slanted on both the left and the right – but neither is ultimately fair," Professor Blake glanced at me for a second, but luckily his gaze didn't linger.

"The advent of the Internet has also radically changed how we report the news," he continued. "These are the days when everyone has a blog and some people actually think that a blog purports truth."

"They don't?" At least another student asked the question this time.

"I'm not saying that they all don't. I'm saying, though, that blogs are not always researched properly," he said. "Most of the time, in fact, they're just opinions. Like movie reviews."

Professor Blake got up and started pacing back and forth at the front of the room. "Let's try a little experiment shall we?"

Not waiting for an answer, he turned back to the class. "How many people here believe in ghosts?"

That's a weird question for a journalism class, I thought. I looked around the room and saw more than half of the hands shoot up. Good grief.

"Good. Put your hands down. Now how many people believe in vampires?"

The same people's hands shot up. I noticed Professor Blake's eyes rest on me for a second. It didn't propel me to raise my hand, even though I'd noticed that Matilda had raised her hand to both questions.

"Okay," he continued. "If Matilda here writes a blog and says that vampires are real, is that news?"

"It depends," I muttered.

"Did you have something to add, Zoe?"

Crap, he'd heard me. I cleared my throat. "I said, that depends." I was never one to shy away from a debate – even if it was about vampires.

"What does it depend on?"

"Whether or not these vampires sparkle." That got a chuckle from everyone in the room except Professor Blake.

"Is it news?" he pressed.

"No."

"Why not?"

"Because there's no proof that vampires exist and you can't print something as truth without proof."

"What if you have proof?"

"Like what? A big pile of dust?"

"What if you capture a vampire?"

"I think if someone caught a vampire then reporters from CNN and ABC would be handling the story – not Journalism 101 students."

Professor Blake frowned at my flippancy. I tossed my hair over my shoulder and met his gaze evenly. I was not going to back down. I didn't care if I failed.

Professor Blake broke from the staring contest first and then turned back to the class. "Is Zoe right?"

Matilda decided now was the right time to jump in. "If I see a vampire, though, and report on my experience that's okay, right? I can even talk to it?"

"What, like *Interview with a Vampire*?" My patience was running thin.

"Maybe," Matilda rolled her eyes at me. I noticed a few people around us giving me dirty looks. I had no idea how I had become the bad guy in this scenario.

"If you did get an interview, what would you ask? What's your favorite blood type?"

Matilda looked slightly distressed. "You don't have to mock me."

"I'm not mocking you." I was totally mocking her. "I just want to see things from your point of view."

"I've seen things," Matilda announced.

"Really? What things?"

"I saw a vampire when I was 16. He was hanging outside of a movie theater."

"Doing what?"

"Trolling for victims."

"How do you know that?"

"Because I saw him sniff the air and follow a girl."

"Did you call the police?"

"And tell them I think I saw a vampire? No, they'd think I was crazy." I knew she was crazy.

"No, did you call the police and tell them there was some strange guy sniffing teenage girls outside the movie theater and following them?"

"Of course not."

I shook my head in disbelief. Matilda decided to change the subject.

"I've also seen ghosts."

"Oh yeah? Did they wear sheets?"

"No, my grandma came to me in my dreams the night she died and told me that she'd always love me, but she had to go."

"How do you know she was a ghost and not an angel?"

"I ... I just know all right."

The room was quiet for a minute as Professor Blake looked around expectantly.

"You've seen a werewolf!" Matilda had jumped to her feet to exclaim this little gem.

"I have not."

"Yes you have," she pointed at me. "That's what that whole Dog Man thing is supposed to be."

"First of all, the Dog Man is supposed to be Bigfoot, not a werewolf, and I never said I saw him. I said that was a local legend. I think that's as much crap as this other stuff."

All the while Matilda and I had been arguing, Professor Blake had been watching me silently. I could feel the confusion – and a certain degree of disappointment – rolling off of him.

I couldn't believe this conversation was actually going on. I also couldn't believe he was letting it go on.

Professor Blake cleared his throat loudly and stepped between Matilda and me. I think he was worried there might be bloodshed – or at least some vigorous hair-pulling.

"Let's call it a day everyone," he said. "For your homework, I want you to try and prove that vampires exist in a news article." He turned to me as he gave the assignment. He was challenging me to protest. I figured I might as well not leave him disappointed.

"We're supposed to prove that vampires exist?"

Professor Blake nodded at me silently. The rest of the class, I noticed, had started talking excitedly to one another as they packed their belongings.

I grabbed my book bag sullenly. I should have left the classroom without saying another word. I didn't, though.

"So, we can use *Twilight* as source material I guess?" With that parting shot, I flounced out of the room.

11 ELEVEN

Despite the unnerving Journalism 101 debacle, I found myself settling into my class schedule pretty easily.

On Thursday, I hadn't had one moment of discomfort. I also hadn't heard from Will – and I'd be damned if I'd call him first.

After classes, I went down to dinner with Paris. We sat with Brittany and Tara – but there was clearly a delineating line being formed in the room. No one was openly hostile to one another – but there was a general sense of unease permeating the atmosphere roiling around the four of us.

Brittany and Tara spent hours each night doing homework. The only homework assignment I had so far was proving vampires existed.

After dinner, Paris and I decided to go to the library to do some research. I had decided to turn my assignment into the joke I knew it was and get quotes from a variety of different vampire books. I could have done it on the Internet, but I was eager to get away from Tara and Brittany.

Unfortunately, Tara and Brittany decided they wanted to check out the library, too. I figured I couldn't get out of it now without looking like a total bitch so I decided to just go with the flow. I could tell Paris was equally agitated by the situation, though.

The sun was close to setting as we left. The days would get shorter and shorter now and soon the sun wouldn't rise until almost 8 a.m. and it would set around 5 p.m. I hated those days – but I couldn't do anything about it until I could afford to move out of Michigan.

The chatter on the way to the library was uninspired – to say the least. Brittany couldn't stop gushing about the fountain of knowledge she was dipping her toe into each day. Tara was equally expressive about her thirst for knowledge – although something rang false in her declarations. I was convinced she was just trying to impress Brittany – although I couldn't figure out why.

Paris and I discussed the state of the *Friday the 13th* franchise. What? It was as good a topic as anything else.

"I liked the remake," she said.

"Good grief. That was awful."

"Those ones from the 80s are so cheesy, though."

"At least they were scary. The new one was an insult. Why would Jason have a pot field?"

"Maybe he likes to mellow out after a kill. Wouldn't you?"

I couldn't argue with that logic.

When we got to the library, Brittany turned to us expectantly.

"What?"

"We have to go to the fourth floor."

"Why?"

"Because that's where the serious studying goes on."

"Who told you that?"

"It's common knowledge."

"From who?"

Brittany shook her head tersely. "Everyone knows that."

Paris stepped between us quickly. "Why don't you and Tara go up to the fourth floor? Zoe and I will meet you up there when we find the reference books we need."

Brittany nodded happily. She clearly had no idea that Paris and I would never make it to the fourth floor – which was apparently full of law books and students that were in desperate need of some sunshine.

Tara and Brittany toted their heavy book bags onto the elevator and waved as the door closed.

"I'm not going to the fourth floor."

"We'll say we couldn't find them," Paris answered smoothly.

"Maybe they'll get lost up there forever?" There was a hopeful note in my voice.

"I wouldn't count on it."

Bummer.

Paris and I loitered around the bottom floor of the library for a while. I selected four vampire books and copied enough quotes to bluff my way through the assignment. Paris leafed through the magazine selection.

When I was done, I turned to her expectantly. "You have anything else you need to do here?"

"No. Why don't we go to the UC for coffee?"

I didn't drink coffee – unless it was half milk and chocolate -- but I agreed to go and wait for Paris outside. No one should be walking alone after dark anyway.

Paris promised she wouldn't take too long and dashed inside the building. I didn't get her coffee excitement – but I was glad she was happy.

I amused myself by walking up and down the sidewalk for a few minutes – all the while trying to avoid the multitude of cracks that marred the cement surface. I wasn't going to take any chances with my mom's back.

After the turn on one trek, I slammed into a dark figure that had been following behind me.

The figure grabbed me to keep me from toppling backwards.

"Sorry," I sputtered. "I didn't hear you behind me."

I looked up to find myself staring into the chocolate eyes of Rafael

— the dark and mysterious stranger from Mike's party almost a full week before.

"What are you doing here?" I'd asked the question before I thought about the intelligence associated with asking it.

Rafael raised his eyebrows briefly as he took in my flustered state. I saw a smile quirk at the corner of his mouth, but he didn't let it take up residence. He lifted up his own cup of coffee, tilting it slightly in case I was blind. "Getting coffee."

I didn't know how to proceed, so I just stood there lamely and looked at him. He looked as good as I remembered. His hair was ridiculously glossy and the moonlight bounced off it like he was a Bond girl or something.

"Why are you out here alone?" I'd watched him scan the area quickly.

"I'm waiting for my roommate."

"Where is she?"

"Inside getting coffee."

"Why didn't you go with her?"

"I didn't want any coffee."

"Still ... ." Rafael pursed his lips undecidedly. Whatever war his mind was waging, he must have picked a side. "It's not safe for you to be out here alone."

I didn't want to tell him I wasn't exactly worried about being jumped. I didn't think he'd get it.

"I'm fine."

"Bad things happen on college campuses," he reprimanded me. "Especially this campus. You're not infallible."

"What do you mean bad things? What bad things?"

My question seemed to take him by surprise. "Nothing. I just mean bad things could happen."

"That's not what you said, though."

"It's what I meant," he practically hissed at me.

"Well, I guess that it is good I'm not your concern then."

Rafael still looked skeptical.

"You can go now." I actually made little shooing motions with my hand. God, I probably was coming across as deranged to him.

"I think I'll wait."

"For what?"

"For your roommate to get back."

"I'm fine."

"Then we'll be fine together."

I gave him my harshest PMS look, but he still didn't back down. I chewed on my lower lip as I regarded him. God, he was so good looking. Too bad he was such a freak.

"So ... ." I was looking for something to talk about. Anything.

"So?" Rafael seemed amused by my discomfort.

"What's your major?" I figured the dumbest conversation ever deserved the dumbest question ever.

Rafael actually let the smile reach his entire face this time. It made him even better looking. He had a dimple in his tan cheeks that was simply spectacular.

"Business."

Hmm.

"What's yours?"

"Probably journalism."

Rafael seemed surprised by my answer. "With Professor Blake?"

"God, no, not with him. He's the one making me doubt my choice."

"Why?" Rafael's question seemed pointed.

"He's just a freak."

Rafael seemed like he wanted to press the issue, but Paris picked that moment to reappear with a coffee in hand. She regarded Rafael with her wide eyes and then smiled warmly at him.

"Hello."

Rafael greeted her back pleasantly. I was surprised he had it in him. Then he launched into an irritating diatribe about women being alone on campus after dark. What a sexist.

"That's definitely something to think about," Paris admitted.

I glared at her. Traitor.

"Well, it is," she said. "You and I are both from small towns. We don't know the dangers out there."

I wanted to smack her – especially when I saw Rafael smiling triumphantly at me. Now I wanted to smack him. I wanted to wipe those dimples right off his face – and then kiss him until they reappeared.

"We'll be going now," I grabbed Paris' arm and started to steer her toward the sidewalk that would lead us back to the dorm. She stopped, though, and looked at it worriedly.

"What?" Could this night get any more exasperating?

"The path is so dark," she murmured.

I shot a death glare in Rafael's direction. He seemed amused.

"I'll walk you home," he offered.

"That's really not necessary," I argued.

"I insist."

Paris turned and grabbed my arm harshly. "If he wants to do it, we should let him."

Crap.

She smiled as Rafael sidled in between us and turned his attention toward her.

"After all, you can never be too careful."

I fell into step behind the two of them. I guess I was wrong. The night actually got worse.

12 TWELVE

When I set up my classes, I was hoping to avoid Fridays. Unfortunately, what they don't tell you when you're registering is that freshmen get last choice in the class department. Unfortunately, I ended up with three Friday classes.

Luckily for me, I breezed through all of the classes that first week – even the increasingly uncomfortable Journalism 101 with Professor Blake. I even managed to avoid eye contact with him throughout the entire class – even when I handed in my vampire piece – which took on such a sarcastic tone in the final version that I was sure I would get a failing grade on it.

When I returned to the dorm, I found Tara and Brittany excitedly chatting about going to Will's fraternity party that night.

I hadn't heard from Will since our blow-up about the mud fight. I wasn't as keen about going to the frat party – but we'd all agreed to go together earlier in the week and I wasn't sure I would be able to gracefully back out of the event. Especially since Will only invited everyone because of me.

"These are exactly the kinds of guys I'm looking for," Brittany told Tara conspiratorially.

"What do you mean?" How Tara could listen to her drivel was beyond me.

"Everyone knows the guys in this frat are from good families, families that have money. These guys are going places."

Brittany's outlook on life was seriously warped, I decided. "Really? Will's family doesn't have a lot of money." For some reason, I was ready to fight with Brittany constantly these days.

"What do you mean?" Brittany didn't seem to believe me.

"His family. They're not well-off. They're not poor, but they're not well-off either."

"Maybe they just don't let you in on their financial situation because they're worried you're a gold digger."

Wench.

"Maybe," I agreed sarcastically. "Of course, Will's dad lives in a trailer in the middle of nowhere and his mom spent the entire summer living in a tent in the backyard with some Indian from the reservation in Traverse City. They even built a ceremonial teepee."

Why I felt the need to air Will's dirty laundry was beyond me. In actuality, we had laughed about the situation with his mother all summer – but I could tell, deep down, it embarrassed him.

"Native American," Brittany responded primly.

"What?" I was getting exasperated.

"Native American. You can't call them Indians anymore."

Tara could tell things were about to get ugly because she stepped in quickly. "Paris wants us to meet her downstairs for dinner."

I turned on my heel immediately after Tara spoke. I couldn't get away from Brittany quick enough. I knew when I found myself hoping one of Will's fraternity brothers gave her herpes that I was letting her get to me far too much. I didn't know how to solve the situation, though. I couldn't exactly banish her from the room – and I didn't know the area well enough to successfully hide a body. I was still fuming about the situation when we made it to the cafeteria.

I separated from Tara and Brittany to get my food. When I sat down next to Paris, she could tell something was wrong. A look from

Tara, though, told her now was probably not the right time to question me about my anger.

Conversation at the table was decidedly stressed throughout the meal. I kept catching Brittany casting me furtive looks throughout. I decided to take the high road; I just pretended she wasn't there.

After dinner, Paris and I managed to put enough distance between us and Tara and Brittany to get on a separate elevator.

"What happened?"

I told Paris what Brittany had said. She didn't seem half as pissed off as I wanted her to be.

"You're overreacting,' she said.

"Excuse me?"

"She's naïve. She doesn't understand how the world really is. When she finds out all these grand things she thinks are going to happen to her aren't really going to happen, she's going to be bitter."

"I hope she's bitter with herpes."

"You can't get rid of herpes," Paris chided me. "She can learn just as important of a message with Chlamydia – and that can be knocked right out of you with a couple doses of penicillin."

I wondered – briefly – how Paris knew that. Then I decided to let it go. I'd only known Paris for a week. There's such a thing as too much personal information.

Paris and I showered first and then went to get ready for the party in the other room. Tara and Brittany showered after us – but there was still a marked tension in the air when they came into the bedroom to get dressed.

I pointedly ignored both of them while I shrugged into a vintage *Star Wars* shirt, jeans, DC Comics Wonder Woman shoes and a Star Wars hoodie.

I turned in time to see Brittany frowning at my outfit.

"You're not going to wear that are you?"

"Why?" I was just itching for a fight.

"You look like a boy."

"What boy would wear Wonder Woman shoes?"

"Well," Brittany bit her lower lip. "You still look like a boy."

"Why does it matter?" I wanted to tell her no boy would wear pants so tight there was worry about the seam ripping, but I didn't think that would get me anywhere.

"You're never going to attract a guy looking like that."

"She already has a guy." Tara looked confused.

"Yeah, but it's not like they're getting along. It's only a matter of time until they break up."

Paris stepped into my path to stop me from stalking over to Brittany and ripping her head off her shoulders. "It's not worth it," she sighed. "She's just trying to bait you."

"It's working."

I listened to Paris' advice, though, and turned my back on Brittany. Screw Chlamydia. I was back to hoping she'd get herpes.

Whether in a show of solidarity or not, Paris dressed in a pair of jeans, a Strokes T-shirt and brown Converse – so her outfit mirrored mine in a weird way. I saw Brittany frown when she saw us standing together – but she wisely chose to keep her mouth shut.

We decided to walk to the party so everyone could have a good time. It was only a half-hour walk and the weather was still nice enough where it wasn't going to be a factor. We weren't going to have to implement designated drivers for at least a month.

Paris and I took the lead on our trek – mostly because I was the only one that knew where the frat house was located.

Before we knew it, we were a good block ahead of Tara and Brittany. I figured that was by their design so they could gossip about us.

"You have to stop letting her get to you," Paris admonished me. "She's doing it on purpose. She thinks you're unbalanced."

"I am unbalanced."

"Yeah, but if it comes down to a fight and we have to get the resident aide involved, then you're not going to want to be the one that comes off as deranged."

She had a point there.

Paris was quiet for a minute, but I could tell she wanted to ask me a question.

"Do you think you're going to break up with Will?"

The question surprised me on some level – but it didn't on others.

"I don't know," I admitted honestly. "I thought all our problems were because we were apart so much. Now it turns out they are because he's a dick."

Paris laughed. "I don't understand why he freaked out that way."

"Me either. I don't have the energy to constantly worry about hurting his feelings or embarrassing him, though."

"Yeah," Paris was staring at the crescent moon. I knew what she was thinking about.

"Are you going to break up with Mike?"

"Yeah, I think so."

"Are you sad about it?"

"If you would have asked me a week ago, I would have been broken-hearted."

"And now?"

"Now I'm just anxious about doing it. Then I think I'm going to be relieved."

"How long will you wait to go after Mark?"

Paris turned to me in surprise. She looked like she was going to argue the point with me and then, instead, shrugged her shoulders and giggled. "That obvious, huh?"

"I don't think anyone else has noticed. I've just been with you guys more."

"Yeah?"

"Yeah."

"He's cool, don't you think?" She seemed desperate for my approval.

"He is cool," I agreed. "I like that he's himself and he doesn't feel the need to impress anyone else."

"Me, too."

Paris and I finished the walk to Will's fraternity house while discussing the pros and cons of dating Mark. Personally, I couldn't figure out how they were both going to fit on that skateboard to go to the movies – but that wasn't really my concern.

When we turned the corner to the frat house you could hear music from almost a block away. Behind us, Brittany squealed with delight when she caught sight of the group of guys on the front porch of the house.

"Aren't they hot?"

I couldn't hear Tara's response – but I was sure she was agreeing with Brittany.

Paris and I exchanged eye rolls. I noticed Will was one of the guys out on the front porch. He caught sight of me as I turned on the sidewalk. He smiled warmly and flew down the steps to give me a hug. I was surprised.

"I'm glad you came," he said. "I wasn't sure if ... ."

"I said I was." I wanted to be annoyed with him, I really did. However, I was merely relieved that he didn't' seem to be harboring any ill will toward me. That made me annoyed with myself – but only for a few seconds.

Will took my hand and led me up the steps. I grabbed Paris' arm and dragged her behind me. I was not going to be stuck with these guys without someone interesting to talk to.

I noticed Brittany glaring at me as Will led Paris and I to the group of guys he'd been talking to. I could feel the jealousy roiling off her. I bit back the urge to stick out my tongue at her and spent twenty minutes pretending to be interested in Will's conversation with his fraternity brothers instead.

After a while, though, I couldn't feign interest in the latest edition of *Guitar Hero* so Paris and I left to refill our glasses at the keg. It was such a nice night; we made our way out to the backyard and seated ourselves in some lawn chairs to talk.

"Is this what a fraternity party is really like?" So far I was unimpressed.

"It might be more fun if you were on the prowl like Brittany," Paris offered.

"Good point."

Paris and I lapsed into an easy silence as we watched party guests flitter about. It occurred to me that there were about twice as many men as women at the party. I thought that was odd.

"Don't you think it's weird that it's such a sausage fest?"

Paris furrowed her eyebrow and turned to where I was looking. "I guess I hadn't thought about it ... but you're right. There are a lot more guys here than girls."

"I thought these were supposed to be the hottest guys on campus, wouldn't the girls be here drooling over them?"

"I don't know. Maybe there's another party we don't know about?"

"Maybe."

I noticed that two of the frat brothers were now positioning themselves near an obviously drunk girl. One was freaking her from behind and the other was trying to isolate her from the front. Before the girl realized what was happening, the guys had managed to separate her from the small group of friends she'd been talking to only a few minutes before.

I started to get up and then stopped. What was I going to do? I really had no reason to get involved. Still, something was bothering me about the situation.

Paris seemed as helpless as I did. "Should we do something?"

"What? They're not technically doing anything. They're just dancing."

Paris nodded, but I could tell she wasn't convinced. I noticed her line of vision, though, had shifted. She saw me looking at her and quickly tried to pretend she had been looking in a different direction. I wasn't falling for that. I followed her sight line to where it had been trained just a few seconds before and found my jaw falling open.

Brittany was still up on the side porch of the house trying to get her fraternity boy, I noticed. Unfortunately, the boy she'd obviously set her sights on was Will. She was hanging on his arm and laughing hysterically. I knew he wasn't that funny. I started toward the porch in a huff.

Paris looked like she wanted to stop me. When she saw the look in my eyes, though, she wisely backed off.

I stomped back up the stairs – pushing myself through the fraternity brothers and their animalistic mating rituals. What was that smell? It smelled like sex? I stopped in front of Brittany and Will with a purpose.

Will seemed to notice me before Brittany and tried to disengage himself from her arms (when had she grown eight of them?). "Zoe," he sputtered. "I was looking for you."

"You were looking hard, I can tell," I didn't want to act like I was jealous, but I was so far gone at this point I couldn't mask my emotions.

Brittany narrowed her eyes as she regarded me. "He shouldn't' have to go looking for you," she announced. "A real girlfriend wouldn't just leave a stud like this alone." She smiled adoringly at Will.

"Stud? Is he a horse now? If you think that, you're going to be sorely disappointed when he gets you into bed."

My remarks were biting – but Will had known me long enough to realize now was not the time to pick a fight he could never win.

Brittany was either too drunk – or too oblivious – to care.

"You should just chill. We're just having a good time."

I noticed she was having a hard time standing up straight. We hadn't been here long enough for her to get that falling down drunk.

"What are you on?"

"What?" Brittany seemed confused.

"What are you on? Acid?" It looked like she was having trouble focusing.

"I would never smoke acid."

I was too concerned about Brittany to completely drop the hammer on her, but I couldn't let her lack of drug knowledge go without commenting. "You drop acid. You don't smoke it." I grabbed her arm and dragged her away from Will – narrowing my eyes at him suspiciously as I did so. "Did one of your frat brothers put something in her drink?"

Will looked genuinely shocked. "Of course not."

Just because Will didn't believe they were capable of such an act didn't convince me.

"We're leaving," I told Brittany pointedly.

"I am not. I'm having a good time." She slurred her words.

"No, we're leaving. I don't care what you want."

Paris had made her way to my side and was grabbing Brittany's other arm.

"Just put her inside and let her sleep it off," Will offered lamely.

"Absolutely not. I don't trust these assholes as far as I can throw them."

I noticed that Aric had arrived on the front porch and was eyeing me curiously. When did he get here? Brittany's sharp intake of breath when she caught sight of him would have been comical at another time. "Who is that?"

I regarded Aric, doubt evident. "He's the guy who's going to help us get home."

If Aric was surprised at my pronouncement he didn't say anything. Instead, he walked toward Brittany and scooped her up in his arms like she weighed nothing.

"Let's go," he made eye contact with me briefly before starting to move off the front porch.

Will was staring at Aric hatefully. He didn't say anything, though. In fact, I noticed that while none of the fraternity brothers seemed happy to see Aric, not one of them was willing to get near him. Instead, the sea of people magically parted as Aric made his way down the steps.

Paris and I followed him quietly. Tara saw that we were leaving and scurried down the steps behind us. "What happened?" She was confused. Where had she been all this time?

"Let's just say Brittany and I are going to have a long talk tomorrow and leave it at that for now?"

Tara nodded in surprise. But, for a second, I saw something darker lurking in the corners of her eyes. Okay, maybe I just imagined that. This whole night was getting weird.

13 THIRTEEN

The walk home was awkward, and Aric didn't even bother with the pretense of idle chatter. I couldn't shut off my inner monologue, though.

"What's up with your fraternity brothers?" Apparently I couldn't shut off my outer monologue either.

Aric didn't even bother looking at me. "What do you mean?"

"I mean, what was up with that party? There were like twice as many guys there as girls and it was like they were trying to double up on all the women." I didn't mention that it had smelled like sex to me. I figured that was more of a comment on me than anything else, and I didn't want him to think I was a nymphomaniac or anything.

"It was weird," Paris echoed.

"I didn't even notice." Tara still seemed confused.

"I don't know what you're talking about," Aric answered evasively. Brittany looked like dead weight in his arms, but he wasn't complaining about carrying her so I didn't offer to help.

When we got to the dorms, Paris, Tara, and I extricated Brittany from him.

"I can carry her all the way upstairs," he offered.

"We got it."

Aric shrugged and left without saying goodbye. Why that irked me, I had no idea.

It took us ten minutes to get Brittany up to our dorm room. I didn't bother trying to get her in anything more comfortable than what she was already wearing. Instead I just dumped her on the floor in the main room – making sure she rested on her side in case she had to throw up.

"Shouldn't we put her in bed?" Tara asked nervously.

"We're not strong enough to lift her onto the top bunk and I'm not going to bother anyone to help us. She'll be fine."

Tara must have decided it wasn't worth arguing about because we all went to bed without exchanging another word.

The next morning, Brittany looked like death warmed over and she was sitting in the middle of the floor holding her head when we all got up.

"How are you feeling?" Tara knelt down next to her kindly.

"Like I've been run over."

"How much did you drink?" Paris asked gently.

"I only had one cup."

I pursed my lips. "One cup couldn't have done that to you."

Brittany glared up at me. "Are you calling me a liar?"

"No, just a slut."

Yep. It was time for the fight I'd been warding off for days.

"Excuse me! I am not a slut."

"Then why were you hanging all over my boyfriend?"

Brittany looked confused. "I was not!"

"We all saw you."

Brittany looked to Tara and Paris for support. They both steadfastly avoided her gaze. "I don't even remember talking to Will."

"Really? Then you probably don't remember hanging all over him? Or calling him a stud? Or telling me I was a bad girlfriend because I didn't give him enough attention?"

I was a steamroller at this point.

"No, I don't," Brittany bit her lower lip to keep from crying. Well, that wasn't going to work on me.

"So it was just a coincidence that you wanted a fraternity boy and you decided to hit on mine?"

"I didn't ... I don't ... why would you ... I don't know what you're talking about," Brittany mumbled.

Paris stepped in at this point. "Maybe she was drugged?" She offered.

The thought had actually occurred to me, but I was so infused with righteous indignation right now that I refused to acknowledge the possibility. "You're taking her side?"

Paris straightened as she stood up. "There are no sides."

"Of course there are," I seethed. "There's the side of the room-mate that swooped in to save the slut and that of the slut."

Paris hardened her icy eyes as she registered my anger. "Maybe you should take a walk and let us talk to Brittany."

"Great! Sounds great!" I stormed out of the room, slamming the door behind me as I went. They could all go to hell as far as I was concerned.

I stalked down the hall and was halfway to the elevator before I realized I was still in my flannel boxer shorts and a tank top (without a bra). There was nowhere I could really go.

At the end of the hall I started pacing the small room where the elevator opened. I couldn't believe this was happening.

The elevator dinged and I turned to it expectantly. A dark haired girl with extremely pale skin stepped off. I'd seen her in the hallway before. I had never talked to her, though.

At first, the girl moved past me without saying a word. When she saw I wasn't getting on the elevator, though, she paused. "Are you alright?"

"Compared to what?" I asked bitterly.

The girl took a sip of the coffee she was carrying and regarded me with her solemn blue eyes. "You want to talk about it?"

"About what? What a slut my roommate is?" Or what an idiot I was for thinking this whole Will thing was going to work out?

"Which roommate?"

"What?"

"Which roommate is a slut?"

"Brittany."

The girl looked surprised. "The blonde one?"

I blew out a sigh. "Yeah."

"She doesn't strike me as a slut."

"You know her?"

"No."

"Then how do you know she's not a slut?"

"Because she was calling you one the other day."

"What?" It took every ounce of resolve I had not to stalk right back down the hall and choke Brittany with a tampon.

"She was going on and on about you spending the night with your boyfriend and how you were going to end up pregnant."

"Oh, good grief."

The girl smirked despite my attitude. "I'm Laura," she extended her hand in greeting. I took it without realizing what I was doing.

"I'm Zoe."

"I know. Everyone knows you."

"How?"

"You're not exactly quiet." Well, that was true.

I let out another long suffering sigh and then sank to the floor with my back against the wall. I had nowhere to go -- and I was definitely not going back to the room yet.

Laura sat on the floor next to me and looked at me expectantly. The next thing I knew, I'd unloaded all of my frustrations from the past week on her. I told her about Will. I told her about Brittany. I even told her about my run-ins with Rafael and Aric. The only thing I left out was my weird interaction with Professor Blake.

After listening for about twenty minutes, Laura surprised me with her response. "Sounds like it could be a book."

"What?" Any anger I had been internalizing seemed to have fizzled during my diatribe.

"It sounds like a book," she reiterated.

"I don't get what you mean."

"You're a woman torn between three men. Two are dark and dangerous. One you've known forever, but he's become someone – actually something – that you don't even recognize."

I took in Laura's flushed faced and sparkling eyes and bit back a harsh retort. "Let me guess, you're a romantic?"

"Well, um ... yes," Laura acknowledged.

"Well, let me just clarify things for you," I said matter-of-factly. "This isn't romantic. It's weird. The whole thing is just weird. There are these weird lurking guys ... ."

"Incredibly hot guys," Laura interjected.

"They're still lurking about. If a serial killer is hot he's still a serial killer."

Laura had the grace to look appropriately chastised.

"Then we have the guy I've been with since I was fourteen acting like a freak and living with a bunch of freaks."

Laura wisely let me continue.

"Then there's my very prim roommate who desperately needs to get some, but apparently wants to get some with my boyfriend – a boyfriend that I can't even decide if I want anymore," I finished lamely.

"Things could be worse," Laura offered.

"How?"

"You could be in love with a vampire."

The conversation had taken a decidedly uncomfortable turn. "I'm sorry?"

"You could be in love with a vampire. Like Edward from *Twilight*."

"If I'm going to fall for a guy that sparkles, he better at least look like he bathes," I grumbled.

Laura ignored my snarkiness.

"Or poor Dracula. He was just so misunderstood and everyone thought he was a monster and he really had no way to control himself."

"Why are we talking about vampires again?"

"You said things couldn't get much worse," Laura responded.

"And this is your way of showing me just how things could get worse?"

Laura nodded. She seemed so normal a few minutes ago.

"You want breakfast?"

"I already ate."

"Well, I'm getting breakfast."

"I can go with you," Laura was too nice for her own good, but beggars couldn't be choosers at this point.

"Okay, just let me go put a bra on," I said. "If you think people were talking about me before – just wait until I'm the girl that goes to breakfast in a tank top without a bra."

14 FOURTEEN

After breakfast, I decided I still wasn't talking to any of my roommates. I wasn't really angry with them anymore, but I wasn't exactly happy with them either. Internally I could acknowledge that I had been out of line – and perhaps off-base. Externally, though, it was still all their fault.

I opted, instead, to stonily pack up all of my laundry and haul it into the basement with my homework. I figured I could waste most of the afternoon down there without looking like I was running away from a problem. Of course, I was running away from a problem – but I just didn't want to look like I was a big old coward.

I placed my two loads into the machines, sat down in one of the armchairs and pulled out my ereader to read through a chapter for Astronomy class. When I was done, I sat there and pondered what I had just read. All this science stuff was just ridiculous, I decided. I took Astronomy because I thought it would be fun. This was just too much work.

I heard some laughing going on outside the laundry room door so I poked my head out to see what was going on. To my surprise, it was Laura and Mark. Mark was busy skateboarding through the empty meeting room off the adjacent hallway and Laura was watching him while she messed with some clay in the middle of the floor.

I couldn't be sure, but it looked like Laura was making beads or something. Great, a crafty hipster.

I realized that both Mark and Laura had noticed me watching them so I stepped into the room. "I didn't mean to interrupt," I said.

"You're not," Laura said invitingly. "We were just talking."

Mark smiled his slacker greeting but never stopped zipping around the room.

"What were you talking about?" Please don't say vampires. Please don't say vampires.

"*Glee.*"

Just as bad.

"Why would you be talking about *Glee*?"

"We both are fans."

"Why?"

"What do you mean why? It's a great show."

"It's a musical."

"So."

"So, it's a musical."

Laura decided to change the subject. "What shows do you like?"

"I don't watch a lot of television."

Mark took in my *Goonies* T-shirt and looked at me, a question on his face.

"What? I like movies not television."

"So what's your favorite movie?"

"*The Empire Strikes Back.*"

That set the three of us off on a discussion about the state of science fiction today. I lamented that there weren't great shows like *Alien Nation* and *V* anymore, while Mark lauded SyFy's slate of shows.

"They're okay," I offered. "I'm not in love with anything on that network right now, though."

"I love *Once Upon a Time*," Laura giggled. "Prince Charming is so cute."

"I liked the sheriff better," I surprised even myself with that revelation.

"He was cute," Laura smiled encouragingly at me.

"Too bad he died."

The rest of the afternoon flew by. Mark let me have another try on his skateboard – and it was surprisingly easy on the carpet. I wasn't as worried about falling.

Once I'd finished my laundry, Mark and Laura helped me carry it upstairs. When I walked into the dorm room, I found Paris, Tara and Brittany all drinking whiskey sours.

"What's the occasion?"

"Just trying to make Brittany feel better." Paris seemed to be daring me to attack her. Instead, I introduced Laura to everyone in the room and then the three of us joined the three of them for drinks.

"So you decided to solve Brittany's blacking out problem from last night with more liquor?" That didn't seem like a viable solution to me – but I didn't want to start another fight.

"We figured if she drank again she might remember what she forgot last night." Tara's face was flushed. If I had to guess they'd been drinking a good hour before I returned to the room.

"That only works with pot," I offered.

"That's true," Mark agreed. "He seemed to be enjoying his drink, too.

Brittany suddenly turned to me and grabbed my arm securely. "I'm sorry, Zoe."

She seemed so earnest I wanted to hug her for a brief second. Instead I laughed. "I'm sorry, too. I knew something fishy was going on. I shouldn't have attacked you."

"No, I want you to know that I would never purposely go after your boyfriend," tears were actually starting to leak from her eyes. Great. This was all I needed.

"Drink your whiskey sour." It had come out a little gruffer than I wanted, but Brittany got the message and turned back to her drink.

The drinking went on for a good four hours before people started passing out. Paris and Tara were the first to retire to their beds. I could hear both of them breathing regularly, so I knew they would be down until tomorrow morning.

I cut Brittany off around 11 p.m. I knew she'd be regretting this binge tomorrow morning. She grumbled the entire way into the bedroom – shutting the door behind her.

Laura had left a few minutes before – but not before I caught her casting a wistful glance in Mark's direction. I figured that situation between Laura and Paris would come to a head at a future date. For now, I decided to ignore it.

When Mark and I were the only ones still up, we decided to toss in a DVD and watch a movie. I opted for *The Empire Strikes Back* and he didn't argue.

We were just finishing up with the planet Hoth assault, when there was a knock at the door. Since it was after midnight, I moved to the door cautiously and peered out the peephole. There was a goofy looking guy with slicked back hair (this isn't *Jersey Shore*, people) and an orange cast to his skin on the other side of the door.

I opened it cautiously.

"Hi, I'm Braden," the boy offered.

I just stared at him without saying a word.

"I'm here to see Brittany."

"She's asleep."

"She just called me." The orange boy looked confused. I figured that was his perpetual state.

"When?"

"Like fifteen minutes ago."

I clenched my jaw and moved away from the confused boy in the door. As he started to step in I whipped around. "Stay!" I then turned back to the bedroom and opened the door. Brittany was standing on the other side excitedly.

"Is that Braden?" She whispered.

"Yes. Why did you call him?"

"I figured it was time." I noticed Brittany was leaning on the desk so she wouldn't fall over.

"Time for what?"

"To turn in my V-card."

"What's a V-card?"

"My virginity," Brittany hissed.

"Wait, so you drunk dialed him and called him over to take your virginity?"

"Yes."

I can't believe this. "Why?"

"I just want it to be over with."

I sighed. Brittany was just too much work. "Go to bed."

Brittany looked confused.

"I said go to bed. You're not turning in your V-card tonight."

"Why not?" Brittany pouted.

"Because you're not going to remember it tomorrow and you'll most probably regret it in the morning. If you're going to do this – which I recommend by the way – then you should be sober." What I didn't add is that she should also be prepared. I doubted Brittany was the type of girl to carry condoms around, and Braden looked too goofy to have anything but an expired one in his wallet.

Brittany looked like she was going to argue. Instead, the liquor seemed to be getting the better of her and she crawled into her bunk.

"Tell Braden I'll call him tomorrow," she murmured into her pillow.

"I will." I had a few things I was going to add to that message – but she didn't need to know that.

I walked back out into the common room, pulling the bedroom door shut behind me as I did. "Brittany won't be coming out to play tonight."

Braden looked nonplussed. "Why not?"

"I put her to bed."

"Maybe if you just let me see her ... ?" Braden obviously wanted to dip his wick. I could tell he was trying to decide how much of an obstacle I would be. *He had no idea.*

"You're not going to see her. You're going to leave here. You're going to forget she ever called you. Oh, and you're going to think long and hard about what a piece of shit you are."

"Excuse me," Braden took a menacing step into the room.

I strode across the floor and stood toe-to-toe with him. His persona had gone from goofy to dangerous pretty quickly, I noted. I had no intention of backing down, though. I needed to bitch at someone – and he was as good a person as anybody.

"Who do you think you are?" Braden growled.

"I'm your worst nightmare," I responded. "I'm the person that knows what kind of person you are. The type that would take advantage of a drunk girl and never talk to her again. I'm also the type of person that can hold her liquor so you can't bamboozle me."

I stepped sideways at that point and opened the door wider as I gestured for Braden to leave.

"Now, Braden, you are going to leave."

"What if I don't?" The question seemed like he asked it with a dose of courage, but I could tell he was a coward.

"Well, if you don't, then I'll start you on fire and we'll just go from there."

Braden met my gaze evenly – I'll give him props for that – but he must not have liked what he saw there. He quickly slipped out the door and hurried down the hall. If I was a better person, I'd put one hundred dollars on the fact that he looked back to make sure I wasn't following him at some point. I didn't look, though.

Mark was shaking with silent laughter when I turned back around.

"What?"

"You're just one scary bitch."

"And don't you forget it," I grumbled as I threw myself back in the chair and tuned back in to a galaxy far, far away.

15 FIFTEEN

The next morning was a rough one for all of us. I wasn't technically hung over – but I was still pissed at Brittany's antics.

While Brittany was in taking the longest shower known to man, I filled Paris and Tara in on what had happened after they went to bed.

To my surprise, Paris found the situation hilarious. "I'm sorry, but that is just so ... so Brittany," she sputtered.

"What did the guy do when you threatened to start him on fire?" Tara seemed concerned.

"What do you think he did? He left."

"But you weren't really going to start him on fire were you?"

"Probably not. It depends on how obnoxious he got."

After breakfast, Paris said she wanted to go back to the library. Since I didn't want to hang around with a complaining Brittany, I agreed. She hadn't brought up the Braden situation from the night before, but I was just betting she was waiting for me to leave the bedroom before she called him to apologize for my misbehavior.

As we headed toward the library, Paris seemed to be in a chatty mood.

"Do you think Brittany was drugged at the party?"

Since we'd been fighting the day before, we really hadn't discussed the situation.

"I don't know, but I don't think she drank enough to be that out of it."

"Have you talked to Will?"

"No."

"Are you going to?"

"I don't know."

"Do you think he knew she was drugged?"

That was a good question. All my years with Will would lead me to believe he wasn't capable of that. He was different at college, though. I had to admit that. Was he that different, though?

"I don't think he knew she was drugged," I finally said. "I can't believe he'd condone that."

Paris nodded quietly. "What are you going to say to him?"

"I don't know," I answered truthfully. "I feel like ... I feel like we're floundering but ... ." I didn't know how to finish the sentence.

"But you don't know if you want to throw four years away just because the first week of college hasn't been what you suspected," Paris supplied.

I blew out a sigh. Paris had hit the nail on the head there. "It's so weird. We had a great summer. It was like the best summer ever. Now, though, I just don't know."

"Do you love him?"

"I don't know. I keep saying that. I used to think I did, but now it's just like we're going through the motions. Neither one of us wants to be the bad guy to end things."

Paris was silent. She just let me talk.

"I don't understand how things could go from good to bad so quickly."

"Maybe they were never really that good."

"What do you mean?"

"Maybe you just thought they were good because you were

having so much fun. Maybe, because it was summer, you thought that going to concerts and kayaking and barbecues meant that your relationship was healthy when it wasn't."

I realized she wasn't just talking about my relationship. "Is that how you feel about Mike?"

"Yes." Paris' succinct answer took me by surprise.

"When are you going to break up with him?"

"Soon."

"How soon."

Paris met my eyes evenly. "Very soon. I just have to work up the courage."

We lapsed into silence again. I admired Paris' strength. I wasn't sure I was at that point yet.

"We weren't together for four years, though," she offered. I could tell she was trying to give me a way out.

"How long were you together?"

"About nine months."

"Still, that's a long time."

"It is. It's not four years."

"No, it's not four years."

"No one says you have to break up with him," I knew Paris was trying to help. "Maybe you could suggest seeing other people and still seeing each other?"

I bit my lower lip in worry. "Maybe, but what's the point of that?"

Paris looked at me seriously. "That you're just not ready for him to be completely out of your life?"

"I don't know. I feel like I'm ready to say goodbye but then, when I think about never waking up and seeing him next to me again, I feel like crying."

Paris nodded sympathetically.

"Of course, I've also imagined smothering him in his sleep twice in the last week."

Paris couldn't help but laugh. "That would be a whole other way to go."

I shrugged. "I'm not going to do anything until it feels right."

"What if it never feels right?"

The question took me by surprise. Was that even possible?

We made the rest of the trip to the library in relative silence. We both had our own problems on our mind. As we approached the library, I noticed that a small throng of people were grouped together off to the side – and they seemed excited.

"What's going on?"

"I don't know."

Paris and I both inched over to the group to see what had attracted everyone's attention. I don't know what I was expecting, but this wasn't it.

"You are a worthless slut!"

In the middle of the group was a tall, willowy boy that would look innocent in any situation but the one he currently found himself in. His backwards baseball cap, Detroit Tigers' T-shirt and baggy canvas pants belied a teenager. His angry words belied a raging man.

I looked to see whom he was talking to and was surprised to see it was a tiny girl with mousy brown hair and doe-like eyes. She was shrinking away from the boy in fear.

"I told you I don't know what happened," her lower lip was quivering. "I don't remember what happened."

"Well, let me fill in the blanks for you," the boy said. "You went to an Alpha Chi party and slept with half the brothers there."

Paris and I raised our eyebrows at each other.

"I don't remember that. I told you. I was drugged or something." The girl was weeping at this point. She looked lost.

"That's a little too convenient for my taste," the boy said bitterly. "I can't believe that after everything we've been through you'd go to a party and do ... that!"

"I told you I don't remember anything," the girl pleaded. "Why won't you believe me?"

"Because your roommates told me that you went to bed with two different guys."

"Nice roommates," I muttered under my breath to Paris. She merely nodded. She couldn't tear her gaze away from the scene playing out in front of us.

"I told you, I think I was drugged," the girl didn't seem sure if she believed her own excuse. I believed her, though. That was the same party Brittany had went goofy at.

The boy grabbed the girl's arm roughly and shook her. "I don't believe you."

Without even thinking, I pushed my way through the crowd and dragged the sobbing girl away from the boy. "Leave her alone."

I looked the girl over to make sure he hadn't hurt her. She seemed emotionally spent.

"Mind your own business, bitch."

I turned to the boy with my own sense of rage. He seemed surprised by my reaction and took an involuntary step back. I didn't blame him.

"It is my business when you start shaking your girlfriend like a rag doll."

"She's a slut."

"Well, you're stupid. Does that mean I can beat the shit out of you?"

"Like you could," the boy was playing up to the group of friends that were standing behind him. He looked a little scared of me, though.

I turned my attention back to the girl. "Are you okay?"

She nodded mutely, but I could see her lower lip was starting to quiver again. Great, more crying.

"Apologize to her," I ordered the boy.

"No."

"You don't hurt your girlfriend. And you most certainly don't get away with it without at least apologizing."

"I'm not apologizing for nothing."

"Anything," I snapped back.

"What?"

"If you're going to be an asshole, at least do it with proper grammar."

The boy stepped toward me, clenching his fists. I didn't know if he was going to hit me. I wasn't going to wait to find out, though. Without even thinking, I raised my right knee and slammed it into his groin.

The boy doubled over in pain – and every guy in the crowd had a sharp intake of breath at my actions. I wasn't done though. While the boy was distracted I then grabbed the back of his head and slammed my knee up into his face – causing him to fall backwards onto the ground.

His friends looked like they wanted to come to his aid – but there was no rationale for five guys attacking a girl. Instead they knelt beside him, all the while casting wary glances in my direction.

I could feel everyone that had amassed in the little group looking at me. The boys were shooting me hateful glances as they gathered their friend and dragged him off. The girls were looking at me admiringly.

There was one other set of eyes, though, that I couldn't read. I could feel them, though. I turned defiantly to see who was giving me the once-over. I pulled up short, when I realized it was Professor Blake.

We stared at each other for a full minute. I was practically daring him to admonish me. Instead he turned on his heel and walked away. About a hundred yards out, I saw him pause and turn back. The look in his eyes was thoughtful – not belligerent.

16 SIXTEEN

After leaving the library with the distraught girl, Paris and I tried grilling her for more information on the party. Well, actually I tried grilling her. She was sobbing so hard, though, we couldn't understand a word she was saying. What she was uttering sounded like a series of whale calls without the water to filter them.

Paris tried a different approach – cajoling the information out of her – but that didn't work either. Instead, we ended up walking her back to her dorm. Unfortunately, she lived on the other side of campus in one of the all-girl dorms.

On the walk back to Wharton Hall, Paris was thoughtful.

"Do you think they're drugging girls for sex?"

"I don't see why else they'd be drugging them," I responded. "You have to admit, something weird was going on at that party."

"Yeah," Paris looked uncomfortable but she plowed on ahead anyway. "Do you think Will is involved?"

"I don't know," I answered truthfully. "It's not like he's not getting any, though, so I don't know why he'd have to drug anyone."

Paris nodded in silent agreement. "Still," she mused. "He can't be oblivious to what's going on at that place."

"No."

"Are you going to ask him about it?"

"I guess I'm going to have to."

When we got back to the dorm, we wandered through the nearly empty cafeteria before returning to our room. The cafeteria is left open at night for those that want to study. The pop machines and soft-serve ice cream machine are also left on, and Paris and I both indulged with an ice cream cone.

We were at the machine when we heard some random giggling. When we turned around, we found Brittany flirting with several guys from our floor a few tables away.

We went over to the table to join them. When Brittany saw us, I couldn't ignore the angry expression that flitted across her face momentarily. She was probably annoyed that we interrupted her mating session. The rest of the table inhabitants seemed happy to see us, though.

"Hey, Zoe, Paris," Rick No. 1 greeted us amiably. I noticed that Brittany had placed a possessive hand on his arm in an attempt to draw his attention back to her.

"Hey," I greeted him with a wide smile. I could really care less about Rick No. 1 – or No. 2 for that matter – but I'm always up for irritating Brittany.

"Where have you guys been?"

Paris and I told everyone at the table about our night's adventure. I noticed Brittany sit up straighter when we told our story.

"Do you think she was drugged like me?"

"We don't know that you were drugged," I reminded her. "We should have taken you to health services and had you tested. If we were thinking, that's what we would have done. Now we're just working on an assumption."

"We could still go do it," she offered.

"Most date rape drugs are out of your system pretty quickly," I said.

"How do you know?" There was an accusatory tone to her voice that I found grating.

"I watch television."

"Well, we could go anyway," she turned to Rick No. 1 with what I'm assuming was her best seductive look. To me she looked like she was constipated. "Would you walk with us? I'm scared now to be out without a man I can trust."

I snickered under my breath. Rick No. 1 smiled at my amusement, while Brittany shot me her best PMS glare.

"I think Zoe is right," Rick said. "I think it would be a waste of time."

"Oh," Brittany said disappointedly. "We could go back and see if they try to drug me again?"

"That's sounds like a stupid idea," I interjected.

"Excuse me! Did you just call me stupid?"

"No, I said your idea was stupid."

"How do you figure?"

"We can't guarantee that we can control the situation this time like we managed to last time," I said matter-of-factly.

Brittany grudgingly agreed. "Yeah, it would suck if they managed to separate us."

"And I would imagine that would be the first thing they'd try to do – even if they'd let us through the front door."

"Why do you think they focused in on Brittany?" Rick No. 1 asked.

"That's a good question," I said. "I don't know. There were a lot of girls there."

"What if ... ?" Paris looked both thoughtful and reluctant.

"What?"

"I don't know, what if ... ?" Paris took a deep breath, steadying herself. "What if they're targeting virgins?"

Brittany made an embarrassed squeak and shook her head disapprovingly at Paris. I was interested in the theory.

"Why do you think that?"

"Because that guy at the library said that girl was a virgin until she was with those guys," Paris said. "Why would she say no to her boyfriend but yes to strangers?"

"That's a good question."

"Plus, we know Brittany is ... ." Paris broke off when she saw Brittany glaring in her direction.

"Frigid," I offered. I didn't really care about pissing Brittany off.

"Innocent," Paris finally supplied.

Rick No. 1 sniggered as Brittany's face turned a violent shade of red. "Just because I don't sleep with whatever guy pays me any attention – like other people I know – doesn't mean I'm innocent."

"So, what, you do everything but?"

Brittany looked confused.

"If you're not innocent and you haven't had sex that means you're everything but girl."

Brittany still looked confused.

"You know, blow jobs, hand jobs ... rim jobs."

Paris couldn't help herself as she choked on her ice cream she was laughing so hard. Brittany didn't find me as funny.

"You are disgusting," she hissed, getting to her feet dramatically and flouncing from the table.

The guys who had been sitting and listening were also amused by the conversation. Rick No. 1 actually swiped a few tears from his eyes, he was laughing so hard. "I don't think she could ever give a blow job or a rim job," he finally wheezed out.

"Why is that?"

"She'd have to stop talking to do both and I'm not sure that's in her wheelhouse," he laughed.

He could be right.

When Paris and I returned to the room, Brittany and Tara had both retired. Since we had our second week of classes the next day – we opted for the same. Paris wouldn't let me go to bed, though, until I promised to apologize to Brittany the next day.

When we woke up the next morning, I was relieved to find that both Brittany and Tara had already left for class. If I was lucky, Paris would forget about my promise and Brittany would stop being such a pill. I know, a girl can dream, can't she?

My classes were largely uneventful for the day. Even Journalism 101 was relatively relaxed.

When Professor Blake handed my paper back to me I expected to see a big fat F. Instead, he'd given it a ninety-two. He'd even written "highly entertaining" in red ink on the top of the paper.

I noticed Matilda was trying to shove her paper in her bag quickly. She couldn't do it fast enough to hide the eighty prominently marked on the top of her paper. I also saw the notation Professor Blake had etched across the top: "Try using your imagination."

After class, Matilda and I were packing up our belongings and she was seething.

"I can't believe he gave me an eighty."

"It could have been worse," I offered. "That's still well above passing."

"I'm used to getting A's," she said haughtily.

"College isn't high school," I said succinctly.

"I know college isn't high school," she sputtered.

"Well, I'm just saying, we have to adjust our expectations." Of course, I'd put zero effort into mine and still got a ninety-two. I didn't think that was something I should bring up to her, though.

Matilda decided she wanted to talk about something else. "Have you seen Rick lately?"

"We had ice cream together last night."

Matilda furrowed her brow. "Just the two of you?"

"No, just a few people from our floor."

"Is he seeing anybody?"

"I think he's seeing everybody," I said honestly.

"Oh," Matilda looked disappointed. "Does he ever ask about me?"

"No." Now she looked crushed. "Maybe he's gay?"

That notion didn't seem to make Matilda any happier. "Maybe he just doesn't like me."

I bit back my reaction to her little gem of wisdom. I didn't think kicking her when she was down sounded like a good idea. She wasn't Brittany, after all.

We were heading out the door when I heard a voice behind me. It was Professor Blake.

"Ms. Lake, would you stay a moment?"

I froze for a second and then slowly turned to face him. "Why?"

"I want to talk to you about your paper."

Crap.

17 SEVENTEEN

Either Matilda didn't notice my sudden panic about having to stay behind with Professor Blake, or she didn't care. My guess? She didn't care.

"See you later," she waved brightly and walked away. I couldn't help but hope she would trip and crash headfirst into the drinking fountain on her way down the hall.

I turned and faced Professor Blake. This really was my worst nightmare. To my horror, things got worse. Professor Blake motioned for me to sit down at a desk. When I did, he moved to the door and shut it so we were alone inside. Sure, there was a whole hallway of students just a few feet away – but I felt extremely secluded.

"I thought you liked my paper?" I was nervous, but I was fighting to regain some modicum of control so he wouldn't see the fear.

"I don't really want to talk to you about your paper," Professor Blake admitted. "I did find it amusing, though. I would have given you a higher grade, but your punctuation is atrocious."

"Well, then what do you want to talk about?"

Professor Blake was contemplative for a second. He seemed to be having an inner fight with himself. He sat down on the edge of his desk and regarded me.

"I saw you outside the library last night."

"So?" If he was going to try and have me brought up on some sort of charges for kneeing that idiot I was about to get incensed.

"I was impressed."

Well, I wasn't expecting that.

"Not many people would put themselves in harm's way to save a girl they don't know."

"That's more of a commentary on the apathy of our society than me isn't it?" I don't know what I was expecting, but the turn this conversation was taking was even more uncomfortable than I initially predicted.

"Yes, it is," Professor Blake agreed. "Still, you showed great courage in what you did."

"I didn't really think about it. I just reacted."

"Yes, but most people would have reacted by running in the other direction. You ran into danger."

"I didn't really consider him that dangerous."

Professor Blake looked surprised. "Why is that?"

"He's just another mealy-mouthed and pouty virgin. He thinks he's owed something by society. I've found the easiest bullies to bring down are those that get off on hurting women."

"You've faced a situation like this before?"

I hedged. I wasn't sure how to answer that. "I don't know what you mean?"

"You've intervened when a man was beating up a woman before?"

"Just my aunt. She was getting beat up by her husband."

"You mean, your uncle?"

"Not by blood. No. Plus, this was her second husband and she's on her third now. He wasn't around all that long. And, trust me, no one misses him."

Professor Blake smiled a little at my answer.

"Zoe, I'm curious, what do you think about the essay I assigned?"

"I think it was retarded." No reason to lie at this point. He seemed to want to hear the truth.

"And why is that?"

"This is journalism. We're dealing with facts here. We shouldn't be focusing on lame vampire fiction. I can do that in my English literature class."

"I see," Professor Blake seemed to be scrutinizing me a little more than I was comfortable with. "And what if it was true?"

"What if what was true?"

"All of it."

"All of what?"

"Vampires. Werewolves. Ghosts. Witches."

Professor Blake said it with absolutely no guile. I couldn't help but look around to see if I was being caught on some candid camera show.

"What are you doing?"

"Looking for the camera."

"What camera?"

"The one for whatever stupid reality show this has to be a set-up for."

"There's no camera."

"So, you're just randomly crazy?"

Professor Blake didn't seem offended by my disbelief. "Just because someone has different beliefs from you – that doesn't mean they're crazy."

"Believing in vampires does."

Professor Blake seemed to dismiss my statement with a wave of his hand. "No one believes at first."

"At first? You've told other people this? And you still have a job?"

"Zoe, are you telling me you've never seen anything that defies explanation?"

"Just Ashton Kutcher being paid millions of dollars to act," I responded in my usual snarky way. I felt the conversation warranted it. "Oh, and Justin Bieber being considered a musician."

Professor Blake ignored my sarcasm. "Nothing else?"

"Nope." I was being flippant now. I was also trying to figure out the quickest way out of this classroom and away from this situation.

"What about the Dog Man?"

"The Dog Man? You mean the Bigfoot legend up at home?"

"Yes."

"No, I've never seen Bigfoot." Even as I said it I hesitated. The truth was, on my way to work at the local resort this past summer, I had seen something. It was 6 a.m. and I was supposed to have opened the golf course deli fifteen minutes earlier, so I was in a hurry. I was also hung over and – truth be told – maybe still a little stoned from the night before. In an effort to shave time from my commute, I'd taken the back roads that no tourist could ever find, but residents of the area knew all too well. They were windy and dangerous roads – none of which were covered in concrete – but which also shaved ten minutes off my commute. As I rounded one of those curves I was forced to slam on the brakes. There was a large animal in the middle of the road -- and he was staring at my car. I thought at first it was a bear – but there was something off about the animal's dimensions. This animal had a much more pronounced snout and – when it raised up on its hind legs – it was much thinner than any bear I had ever seen. And, I swear this is true, when the animal walked into the trees to disappear, it actually swaggered a little bit.

Professor Blake must have seen my mind working. "So, you have seen Bigfoot?"

"No, I've never seen Bigfoot," I scoffed. "I saw a bear once."

"But, even now, you're not sure it was actually a bear?"

I didn't know how to answer him – so I didn't.

"What if I told you that the area you grew up in was a stronghold? Not for Sasquatch, though, but for Lupins."

"What are Lupins? I mean aside from the professor in Harry Potter?"

My pop culture reference seemed to have initiated an involuntary tic in Professor Blake, because he winked and then scowled. "Lupins are werewolves."

See, I should have seen that coming. "You're so full of shit. Werewolves?"

"Why are you so dismissive of the possibility? All legends start somewhere."

"Every saga has a beginning," I muttered.

"What?"

"Nothing. Just repeating the introduction to one of the Star Wars movies."

"Well, that seems helpful."

I glowered at Professor Blake. "Why are you telling me this?"

"I think you came here for a reason."

"And what reason is that?"

"To join the fight."

"What fight?"

"Against evil."

"You mean werewolves?" I just knew I was being punked.

"Not just werewolves," Professor Blake said gravely.

"Oh, vampires and ghosts, too."

"And witches."

"And witches," I nodded enthusiastically. "And elves and fairies and trolls and gnomes. It's just like *Charmed*."

Professor Blake frowned at my mock enthusiasm.

"This is not a joke. Covenant College is at the center of a war – a war that has been waging for centuries."

"Between werewolves and vampires?"

"Yes."

"Like *Underworld*?"

"Not everything is a movie."

"Right."

Professor Blake took a step toward me. In my panic to get away, I knocked the desk over as I stood and moved a step back.

"I'm not going to hurt you," he admonished.

"Good to know."

"I'm trying to recruit you."

"For what?"

"There are some of us – a very few – that have formed a group to fight these monsters that are taking over our society."

"Really? That's great." I was now convinced this guy was off his rocker. "So, you're trying to form a group to fight the evil. *Like Buffy the Vampire Slayer.*"

Professor Blake looked like he was about to lose his cool.

"It's not like *Buffy the Vampire Slayer*. This is serious. I'm serious. There are real evils out there."

I'd had enough.

"I'm sure there are but, here's the thing, I'm not interested in fighting evil. I'm not even interested in acknowledging evil. I just want to get a degree, go to a few parties and maybe smoke a few joints here or there."

I moved across the room with a purpose now. I wasn't going to let him scare me into staying.

"Quite frankly, Professor Blake, I'm not interested in joining your freaky little Dungeons and Dragons group."

"You're saying no?" Professor Blake looked incredulous.

"Yes, Professor Blake, I'm saying no. *The Avengers* will just have to get along without me." Then, with as much dignity as I could muster, I threw open the door dramatically and stomped out. Professor Blake wisely opted not to follow me.

18 EIGHTEEN

I wanted to discuss what had happened with Paris when I returned to the dorm room, but I decided to let it go. I figured Professor Blake was just a nut and I should pretend the whole conversation had never happened.

When I entered the room, though, it was absolute pandemonium.

Brittany and Tara were both standing toe-to-toe with Paris, and it was obvious they were in the middle of something. I had heard yelling when I was walking down the hall. I just didn't realize it was coming from my room.

"What's going on?" I was fully prepared to back Paris – whatever the argument was about.

"We were just discussing some things," Tara said bitterly.

"What things?"

"The problems we're having in this room," she said.

"And those would be?"

"You two," Brittany piped in.

"Us?"

"Yes, you two and how you act like you're so much better than us."

"When do we do that?"

"Every day."

"You want to be more specific?" I took the opportunity to look Paris up and down. She was standing in front of Brittany and her fists were clenched at her sides. This wouldn't end well if I didn't defuse it quickly.

"You make fun of me for being a virgin."

"No one makes fun of you." Well, at least not to her face.

"Yes, you do."

"Fine," I blew out a sigh. "You're a virgin. It's hilarious. Let's call CBS and see if they need a new sitcom."

"Making fun of me because I'm a virgin is wrong. It's a form of bullying."

Oh, good grief. I was in this now. "Really? And you don't sit around and call Paris and I sluts because we're not virgins?"

"Of course not!" I'd noticed Brittany pause before she answered, though.

"Really? Be honest."

"I don't think you're sluts," she said. "I think you've made a mistake and maybe you want to rethink your take on life."

"And I think you're uptight and maybe you ought to rethink yours."

"What's that supposed to mean?"

"It means that one good orgasm might knock that stick right out of there."

Paris smirked.

"See!" Brittany was practically screeching now. "You think you're better than me because you've had sex!"

"I'm a narcissist. I think I'm better than everyone." Suddenly I was tired. I was tired of this whole thing.

Brittany apparently didn't know what to say to my admission, so she ignored it. "I think we need to come up with some ground rules."

"Really? And what would those be?"

"You and Paris have to stop bullying me."

"Fine."

"What?" Paris was incensed with me now.

"I said fine. We'll stop bullying her about being a virgin – when she stops whining about every little thing we say or do."

"I don't whine."

"You totally whine."

"I do not! Tara do I whine?"

Tara had found something interesting to focus on behind Paris and I. She didn't appear to want to answer Brittany's question.

"I'm done with this conversation," I announced. "I'm going to the library."

"I'll go with you," Paris said.

I grabbed my book bag and regarded the room for a moment. "I'll meet you out by the front door."

Paris nodded and disappeared into the bedroom to gather her stuff. I turned on my heel and left the room without saying another word. Whoever said your college roommates would be your best friends for life was a filthy liar.

Once outside the building, I took a couple of deep breaths to calm myself. I was still keyed up – but I didn't feel like hitting something anymore.

I looked around and realized that the front of the building was completely deserted. This didn't actually surprise me. The five towers of the dorm each had a separate exit. The exit I'd chosen to go out of was on the far side of the building – the one away from campus. There was really no reason for anyone to be out here.

I figured Paris wouldn't look for me outside this door. After a few minutes of quiet, I turned to go back into the building. I figured I'd have to go to the door we usually went out for her to find me.

When I started moving back toward the building, I noticed some furtive movement out of the corner of my eye.

I swiveled quickly to see what it was. All I saw was a grouping of bushes. I narrowed my eyes as I inspected them. Even though I couldn't see anything – I swear I could feel something watching me.

I was still for a full minute and ... nothing. I had just convinced myself that I was seeing things when I saw the bushes move – and not like a breeze was blowing them. I froze again – this time in fear. I could feel imminent danger – and yet I couldn't seem to move.

My eyes were glued on the grouping of bushes for what seemed like an eternity. My muscles were locked and I was mentally ready to run – if I could just unlock my muscles.

Then, it happened. A shadow slowly detached from the bushes. A shadow the size of a mid-sized man. A shadow that was furtively heading in my direction.

I wanted to scream – but no sounds would come out.

I wanted to run – but I was devoid of the ability to move.

I wanted to wake up – but I was suddenly sure this wasn't a dream.

The shadow made a hissing noise as it stepped closer. There were no lights in my general vicinity – but the moon was bright and I could see some pale skin under a mess of black hair. For a second, Professor Blake's odd conversation popped in my head. Then I realized – this was all some hoax on his part.

Suddenly I could move. And boy, was I pissed.

"You had me for a second," I laughed bitterly.

The shadow kept coming toward me.

"Tell Professor Blake his little ploy isn't going to work. I'm not going to play his game."

Still nothing. The shadow was getting closer.

At the last second, still believing it was a prank, I lifted my bag and swung hard. The figure seemed surprised by my movements and staggered to the side.

That's when I caught a glimpse of what looked like some overly white -- and overly long -- teeth poking out from the guy's mouth.

"This isn't funny."

The truth is, despite myself, a little nagging part of me believed that this all could be real. I wasn't ready to give into that little part – yet.

The shadow took advantage of my indecision and jumped me. He moved so fast I didn't have a chance to react.

I hit the ground hard – my breath momentarily knocked out of me.

I didn't lose my wits, though. I brought my knee up from my prone position – trying desperately to hit that one spot on every guy that incapacitates him. I missed.

The shadow was incredibly strong and he pinned me to the ground with relative ease. I kept trying to buck and kick to give myself some leverage – any kind of leverage. I was getting nowhere, though.

Face-to-face, I could see that the shadow was incredibly pale and those teeth – which I hoped I had imagined – were not only real but also terrifying.

The shadow had made very little noise up until this point. Then I heard him make a sort of slurping sound. Well that was just disgusting.

Without even thinking, I felt my fingers brush upon something on my right side. It was a large rock. Without even stopping to think what I was doing, I brought the rock up instinctively and bashed the shadow in the head.

The shadow made another sound – this time a groan of pain – and I took advantage of the situation to shift his weight off me and slip out from under him.

I regained my footing relatively quickly – but my wits were still scattered.

I realized I was in a life or death situation here – and yet I was still hoping there was some sort of rational explanation for what was going on.

The shadow had regained itself and was coming toward me again.

I glanced around, looking for anything I could use as a weapon. My gaze settled on a rake that was propped up against the building. It was my only hope.

I scampered toward the rake – even though I could feel the shadow getting closer to me. When my fingers closed around the tool, I didn't stop to think. I didn't tell myself that I could kill my attacker. I just swung. I swung hard.

There was a sickening crack when the rake hit home. I thought for sure the sound I heard was his skull cracking open.

When I turned, though, I realized the sound I'd actually heard was the handle of the rake breaking off. All I was left with was two feet of wood and nothing on the end to protect myself with.

I grabbed the handle and started wielding it like a knife. I knew there was only one thing left to do. As the shadow advanced on me I plunged the handle down into my attacker's chest.

I was shocked with the ease in which it entered his body.

We both froze.

The shadow met my gaze for just a second and then ... poof. He was gone.

I don't mean he disappeared in thin air. I mean he disintegrated in a pile of ash that fell at my feet.

I was stunned. I'd just killed someone. And, yet, I'd left no body.

The world was swimming in front of my eyes and I sat down hard on the pavement. That's where Paris found me five minutes later. I think I was still in shock.

"What happened?" She looked panicked.

"He lied," I mumbled.

"Who did?"

"It was totally like Buffy."

19 NINETEEN

I t took Paris a full twenty minutes – and a Slurpee -- to get me to focus on her.

"What happened?"

Here was the conundrum: How could I possibly explain what happened without Paris thinking I was crazy.

"It was nothing. I just thought I saw something."

"What did you see?" Paris narrowed her eyes shrewdly.

"I thought it was ... I don't know what I thought it was. It turned out to be nothing."

I could tell Paris didn't believe me – but for some reason she opted not to push me on the subject. We didn't end up going to the library – and instead returned back to our room and went to bed.

The next day, I got up early. My dreams had been troubled and, quite frankly, I was blaming Professor Blake.

I didn't even bother going to breakfast. All I could think about was getting to Blake – even if it meant doing it on an empty stomach.

I checked his classroom first – but there was another class going on. I mentally smacked myself for not realizing that it wasn't actually his classroom. He just borrowed it from time-to-time.

I went to the front of the building and found the directory listing. Professor Blake's office was on the second floor. I was so amped up on adrenaline I took the steps two at a time. He had a lot of explaining to do.

The office hallways were completely different from the classroom hallways. Instead of bland cement floors and walls, the office area was filled with warm chocolate walls and shiny hardwood floors. I wasn't in the mood to admire the décor, though.

I made my way down the hall until I found a placard identifying Professor Blake's office. The door was closed – and I paused for a second. My upbringing told me that when you come across a closed door you knock. The dead guy going to ash the night before told me the exact opposite.

I took a deep breath and threw open the door with such force it ricocheted back and hit the wall behind it with a resounding thunk. Professor Blake looked up in surprise. Luckily he was alone.

"Just what the hell did you do last night?"

For his part, Professor Blake didn't let his surprise at my dramatic entrance drag him away from the papers he was grading. The words pretentious and douche were running through my head.

Professor Blake raised his eyebrows at me briefly, but he didn't speak. That was infuriating.

"I asked you a question."

"My office hours aren't for another hour. Come back then."

"And people say you have no sense of humor."

"Who says that?"

No one had actually said that – but I had thought it a multitude of times. I decided to ignore his question.

"Did you send one of your little friends to take me out last night?" Might as well just go for broke.

Professor Blake looked surprised. He got to his feet and moved toward me. For a second, I thought he was going to try and finish the job. Instead, he moved past me and closed the door. He stopped momentarily as he was walking back toward his desk.

"Define little friend," he said, as he sat back in his seat.

A bevy of nasty insults flooded my brain when he mentioned his little friend, but I figured calling his manhood into question probably wasn't the best way to get the answers I was looking for.

"Umm, let's see, dark greasy hair, black clothes, oh, and murderous intent." Sarcasm seemed like such a better way to go.

"If I'm understanding you correctly, you were attacked?" Professor Blake's nonchalance was beyond infuriating.

"Isn't that what I just said?"

"No, not really."

I had a split-second fantasy of strangling him. Instead, I took a deep breath to calm myself.

Blake motioned to the seats in front of his desk. "Why don't you sit down and start from the beginning."

Instead I threw myself into one of the chairs with a dramatic sigh and then launched into the story from last night. When I got to the part about staking the man and him turning into ash, Professor Blake looked surprised.

"You took him out? Alone? I'm impressed."

"It was a survival instinct. It's not like I had any technique or anything," I muttered bitterly.

"Your instincts are your greatest asset."

"I thought that was my mind."

Despite himself, Professor Blake chuckled. "Your mind could be an asset. The way you use it, though, it's definitely a deficit."

I was pretty sure I had been insulted. I decided to let it slide. "You're saying you didn't send him?"

"I fight against vampires. I don't use them as weapons."

"Vampires? We're back to this again?"

"After last night, you still doubt what I told you?"

He had a point.

"It's just so ... ridiculous."

"That's what I thought, too."

"And now?"

"Now? Now I've expanded my horizons."

He made it sound so easy.

Professor Blake regarded me with his pale blue eyes for a second. "Are you ready to expand yours?"

Oh, good grief.

"Just so you know, this doesn't mean I'm ready to join your cause. I'm just ready to learn more," I cautioned him.

"I guess that is a start."

Professor Blake ushered me out of his office.

"Where are we going?" I was hoping he wasn't some sort of a pervert.

"The athletics building."

"Why?"

"So you can broaden your horizons."

The athletics building was on the other side of campus and Blake offered to drive, but I opted to walk instead.

"Still don't trust me, I see."

"You could be some weird pervert."

"I guess that's smart, from your perspective."

As we walked to the athletics building, Professor Blake kept asking me questions about the attack the night before.

"Is there any way that the vampire could have known you would be out there alone?"

"I don't see how. That wasn't even the door I meant to go out. We were going to the library. I just needed some air."

"You're saying it was coincidence?"

"I don't know what else it could be."

"I have trouble believing in coincidences."

"I have trouble believing in vampires. So I guess we'll just have to agree to disagree."

"For now."

I glanced over at Professor Blake. He seemed lost in thought.

We made the rest of the trek to the athletics building in relative silence. I found there wasn't a lot to say.

When we got there, Professor Blake led me through the building to a locked door. He pulled a card out of his wallet and swiped it through the security panel. He opened the door and waited for me to enter ahead of him.

I took a deep breath and stepped through the doors. I had a weird feeling – just for a moment – that nothing was ever going to be the same again.

20 TWENTY

I don't know what I was expecting on the other side of the doors – but everything looked ridiculously normal.

White halls. Cement walls. Bright lights.

"This is it?"

Professor Blake must have noticed the incredulous tone of my voice. "What were you expecting?"

"I don't know. Hogwarts?"

Professor Blake grimaced. "You need to stop basing all of your life decisions on television."

"I don't. I read books and watch movies, too."

"You're very sarcastic."

"It's my super power."

"Flippant, too."

"I'm multi-talented."

"And massively irritating."

"If you think you're the first person to tell me that, you would be mistaken."

"You always have to have the last word don't you?"

"Look who's talking?"

Professor Blake grunted in displeasure.

I followed him down the winding halls until he reached the room he was obviously looking for. When we entered, I was surprised to see that it was filled with books.

"What is this?"

"The history of the supernatural. It's our research area."

I walked over to the book shelves – which were arranged around a rectangular reading table in the center of the room – and perused the titles.

"Someone actually writes non-fiction vampire books?"

"Through the years. Yes."

"How?"

"For many years, there were people that merely watched the supernatural and didn't do anything to try and stop them."

"Like in the *Highlander* television series? You're Joe Dawson?"

Professor Blake openly glared at me at this point. He was so easy. "I never watched the *Highlander* television series."

"You should. Totally cool. Except the final season. That was crap."

"I'll have to take your word for it."

"I have it on DVD if you want to borrow it."

I didn't turn to look at Professor Blake, but something told me he wasn't thrilled at the prospect of watching *Highlander* DVDs.

"Why did you bring me here? I'm not exactly in the mood to read."

"I figured I would show you everything. It's always smart to start with the practical."

"Well, I'm practically unimpressed. This doesn't prove anything – no matter how old some of these books are."

"Then let's move on," Blake responded crisply. I could tell I was on his last nerve.

I silently followed him out of the room. "Where to next?" I asked brightly.

Professor Blake led me to the staircase and headed down. When we got to the basement level, things looked more like I suspected. It was dark, dreary and cavernous.

"See, now this is more like what I suspected."

"Glad I didn't disappoint you."

We made our way through the hallway, passing by a couple of rooms before Blake stopped in front of a heavily ornate door.

"What's this? The potions lab?"

"Let the Harry Potter stuff go."

"How do you know I was talking about Harry Potter? I could have been referencing something else."

"Are you purposely trying to bait me?" Professor Blake snapped back.

"Sometimes."

"It's working."

"Good."

Professor Blake opened the door and ushered me in. I was surprised by what I found. The room was big. Huge, in fact. There were shelves placed around the room that held a variety of different weapons. And, when I say weapons, we're not talking handguns. Instead I saw a multitude of knives, swords and even a couple different hammer-like objects. The center of the room had gymnastics mats spread out.

"This is the training room."

"Training for what? The Renaissance Festival?"

"Combat."

"Combat with who?"

"Supernaturals."

"Vampires?"

"And werewolves."

"Right. Werewolves." My voice was laced with sarcasm. I knew I should probably try to refrain from antagonizing Professor Blake too much – and yet my natural instincts were to continue pushing him.

"I don't understand why this is so hard for you," Professor Blake seemed perplexed.

"You don't understand why it is so hard for me to idly chat about fighting vampires and werewolves?"

"You come from an area that is infested with werewolves. They even wrote a song about it."

"That song is about Bigfoot."

"No, that song is about dog men."

"So, you're saying that werewolves exist and Bigfoot doesn't?"

Professor Blake seemed genuinely surprised by the question. "That's actually a good point."

"Wait, so Bigfoot is real?"

"Anything is possible."

I thought about his answer for a second. After what I'd seen the night before, I guess I could believe that.

"So, someone here actually trains people to fight vampires?"

"We have a lot of trainers. You must keep in mind, it's not just vampires. There are different ways to kill different supernatural species."

"Like what?"

"Obviously you've figured out a stake to the heart kills a vampire. But there are other ways."

"Like what?"

"I couldn't possibly go into all the different ways. We have classes to teach this."

"Classes?"

"Yes. Classes."

"Great. More classes. Sounds like tons of fun."

"There's one more thing I want you to see."

I followed Blake out of the room and down the dark hall again. We didn't have far to go. Two doors down Blake knocked and then opened the door. I was surprised by what I saw inside. There were twenty different students sitting at desks and watching a woman as she lectured from the front of the room.

"Professor Blake," the woman greeted him with a flirtatious smile.

I took in the woman for a second. She looked young. Mid-twenties, at the most. She had long auburn hair that was swept up into a messy bun at the nape of her neck. She also had a round and appealing face that broke into a wide smile when she saw Professor Blake.

"Hello, Professor Worth. I just wanted to bring a new candidate by to see what we do."

I didn't recognize any of the students in the class – who were mostly boys – but they all sat up straighter as they regarded me. None of them seemed impressed.

"This must be Zoe Lake," Professor Worth said by way of greeting. "I've heard a lot about you."

"You have?"

Professor Worth looked surprised by my question. "Of course ... ." She looked conflicted. "You have a great pedigree."

"I'm sorry, what does that mean?"

Professor Blake shook his head at Professor Worth and then turned to me. "I think she has you confused with someone else."

"She knew my name."

Professor Blake glared at Professor Worth for a second. "We have several candidates. She just must have confused your name with someone else's information."

"You're lying."

The rest of the students gasped in surprise. I guess they weren't used to anyone questioning Professor Blake.

"I'm not lying."

"You're not even very good at it. For someone leading a covert group of monster hunters, you'd think you'd be better at lying."

"Can we take this outside?"

"No."

"What?"

"I'm done. I'm not listening to any more of your crap. This is a weird place. You're a weird guy. This is all just ... ridiculous."

I swung around and stormed out of the room. The minute I left I could hear the students murmuring amongst themselves.

I moved quickly down the hall. I could hear Professor Blake saying something to my back as I left, but I ignored him.

I made my way out of the building, exiting the athletics center from the first door I could find. I was surprised when I left. It was dark. I'd spent the entire day with Professor Blake and his lies.

My stomach rumbled. I'd also spent the entire day without eating anything.

I started toward the dorms – the whole time internally lambasting myself for falling for Professor Blake and his lies. There was definitely something going on at Covenant College, but I wasn't going to ally myself with a bunch of liars to figure out what that was. Professor Worth's comments about my pedigree were also frustrating. What did she mean by that?

I was so engrossed in my own thoughts I didn't notice a shadowy figure appear on the sidewalk in front of me. I slammed into him.

The figure grabbed my shoulders to keep me from falling backwards.

"Sorry," I sputtered.

"No problem."

I recognized the voice.

"Rafael?"

"Zoe."

"What are you doing out here?"

"What are you doing out here?"

"Walking back to the dorms."

"Where are you coming from?"

"The athletics center." I didn't see any reason to lie.

"What were you doing there?" Rafael's eyes had narrowed as he waited for my answer.

"Working out."

Rafael regarded me for a moment, taking in my jeans and hoodie, and then shook his head slightly. "You worked out in that?"

"Why do you care?"

"Just curious."

He was lying. For a second, I wondered if he knew what was really going on at the activities center. Then another thought crossed my mind. His cold skin. The fact that I'd only seen him after dark.

"Oh crap. You're a vampire!"

Rafael looked surprised – but only for a second.

"That's a weird thing to say."

"You're not denying it."

"You think I look like a vampire?"

"Well, you're not sparkling or anything."

Rafael didn't respond.

"How are you so tan if you're a vampire?"

"I'm from Spain. It was summer when I was turned." He wasn't trying to hide anything now.

"When was that?"

"A while ago."

"Vague much?"

"I don't know you."

"So, if you knew me you would tell me?"

"Depends," he smiled. God his dimples were cute. "If I decide you're trustworthy."

"Why aren't you trying to eat me?"

Rafael looked surprised. "I'm not hungry." I think he thought I was joking.

"So you're not mindless eating machines?"

"That would be Great White sharks – not vampires."

I furrowed my brow in surprise. "Great White sharks?"

"I like *Shark Week*. You can learn a lot."

Crap. I liked *Shark Week*, too.

"The vampire I met last night tried to eat me."

Rafael looked surprised by this. His arm shot out and he grabbed my wrist harshly. "What happened?"

"Ow," I tried to pull my arm away from him.

"What happened?" I felt like his gaze was trying to bore through me.

"What is your deal?"

Rafael looked surprised. He let go of my wrist reluctantly. This time, when he asked the question, his voice had softened. "What happened?"

I told him an abbreviated version of the story, my gaze never leaving his face.

A miasma of emotions seemed to pass over Rafael's face as I told my tale, but he never interrupted me. When I was done he finally spoke. "You need to be careful."

"What?"

"You're getting a lot of attention on campus."

"Why?"

"I don't know. Don't you?"

The comment about my pedigree flooded through my mind for a second, but I decided not to tell Rafael about that. He was a vampire, after all. "I'm just a girl."

"You're more than just a girl."

"What am I then?"

"I don't know. You just need to be careful."

Rafael walked me back to the dorms. No matter how many questions I asked him, though, he refused to answer any more of them. He didn't even say goodbye when he dropped me off at the front door.

As I watched him leave, though, I noticed that he was prowling around the parking lot like he was hunting. I wondered if he was looking for dinner – or more rogue vampires. I could only hope it was the vampires.

21 TWENTY-ONE

The next morning I woke up with a sick feeling in the pit of my stomach. What was supposed to be a simple, fun and exciting time in my life had turned into a huge clusterfuck.

I went to breakfast with Paris – but I wasn't exactly chatty. My mood was dark and dour. She noticed.

"Where were you all day yesterday?"

"Classes."

"Really?"

"Yeah."

I wanted to tell Paris everything that had happened, but I didn't even know where to start. Plus, there was always the concern that she wouldn't believe me.

"What are you doing today?"

I sucked down some pop. I had a feeling I would need the caffeine.

"Just classes."

"You want to meet at the UC for coffee afterwards?"

"Sure."

That would at least give me more time to think about what I should say to Paris – and how.

We walked to class together in a comfortable silence. I could tell Paris wanted to grill me, but she was oddly silent. Finally, she said something.

"You weren't raped or anything were you?"

The question stunned me. "What?"

"You've been weird since I found you in the parking lot last night. I'm worried that something happened to you."

Something had definitely happened to me -- just not that. "No, I wasn't raped."

"Have you talked to Will?"

"No. Have you talked to Mike?"

"No."

"Are you still going to?"

"Yeah. I just don't know what to say."

"Just be honest." Look at me giving advice, when my own life was falling apart around me.

"Are you still going to talk to Will?"

"I don't know." I was being honest. Everything had changed over the course of the past two days. I didn't know if I could take anything else in my world shifting.

We separated when we got to the building. I went to my first class of the day and essentially zoned out through the entire thing. I tried to listen during my astronomy class with Paris – but I didn't have a lot of luck there, either. My next class was Journalism 101 with Professor Blake. I definitely wasn't looking forward to that.

I plodded down the hallway, dragging the trip to the classroom out as long as possible. I'm not one of those people that rips the Band-Aid off. I feel the need to prod and cajole it for a while. When I entered, Matilda waved excitedly when she saw me. "How are things?"

"Fine." I really wasn't in the mood for her particular brand of enthusiasm today.

"Have you seen ... ?"

I cut her off. I couldn't listen to her Rick No. 1 infatuation any longer. "No. I haven't seen Rick in the past two days."

"Not at all?" She seemed concerned.

"I've been busy."

The class went silent as Professor Blake entered the room. I saw him check my usual seat to make sure I was there, but then he ignored me for the rest of class. He thankfully stayed away from any paranormal assignments as well.

After class, I found myself lingering and I couldn't explain why.

Professor Blake noticed as well. "Do you need something?"

I looked around. The rest of the classroom was empty. Even Matilda had left. I figured she had caught on to my irritated attitude (thank the Force for small favors) and wisely decided to avoid a tense walk back to the dorms with me.

I opened my mouth to answer Professor Blake and then snapped it shut. I honestly didn't know what to say.

"Let's go to my office."

I don't know why I followed him, but I did. The walk to his office on the second floor was made in complete silence -- an uncomfortable silence at that. When we made it to his office, Professor Blake unlocked it and then held the door open for me. I walked in silently. He shut the door behind us.

"I wasn't sure I would see you in class today," he admitted.

"I'm here for an education. I'm not going to let anyone derail that. Not even you."

"I'm sorry about how things went yesterday."

"What, exactly, are you sorry about? That you purposely took me into that place to make me uncomfortable or that you're keeping something from me?"

Professor Blake sighed. "You just have to be combative, don't you? I shouldn't be surprised."

"See! That's what I'm talking about. You have to be cryptic and talk down to me like I'm twelve."

"I'm not talking down to you. You must understand, though, that you're young. You're new to this. There is so much you don't know." Professor Blake gazed out his office window before continuing. "Why are you here? I thought you were done with us."

"Maybe I want to know more."

"Did something happen last night?"

I thought about telling him about Rafael, but something deep inside me told me that wasn't the smart way to go. "No. I made it home fine."

"Then why, all of a sudden, do you want to know more?"

"Two nights ago I was attacked in the parking lot. I killed a man."

"You killed a vampire."

"I killed a man and he turned to ash. I want to know why that happened."

"I don't know why that happened."

"Why does everyone on this campus seem to think they know something about me?"

"I'm sure I don't know what you mean."

"Do not lie to me," I seethed. "You're bad at it and I'm sick of your shit."

Professor Blake sighed. "People think you already know about the supernatural because of where you come from."

"This Dog Man thing again?"

"It's hard to believe you grew up in that small town – a town filled with werewolves – and you don't know anything."

"How do you know it's full of werewolves?"

"I've been there."

"When?"

"Several times."

"When was the last time?"

"Last November."

I wracked my brain, but I couldn't think of anything that stood out from last November. "Why were you there last November?"

"What do you remember about last November?"

"Homecoming."

Professor Blake snorted derisively. "What else?"

I thought for a moment. "Not much. It snowed early. We got to go skiing on the first day of deer season."

"They cancelled school?"

"No. We always get the first day of deer season off. The boys go hunting. The girls go shopping usually. But since we got snow a bunch of us went skiing instead."

"What else?"

"What do you mean? There was nothing else."

"There was something."

I thought some more. "One of my classmates died in a hunting accident," I finally said. "Conner Dalton. He was out hunting with a bunch of friends and he accidentally got shot."

Professor Blake nodded slowly.

"That's what you were talking about?"

"Yes."

"Are you saying Conner wasn't killed in a hunting accident?"

"That's exactly what I'm saying."

"So what killed him?"

"A werewolf."

I was silent for a moment. My heart was racing, though. "How do you know that?"

"The signs were unmistakable. He was mauled by an animal -- a big animal. You don't have bears. So what else could it have been?"

"Why were you there?"

"To handle the situation."

"Meaning?"

"I had to make sure that Conner stayed dead."

"What do you mean?" I felt like I was swimming in quicksand sometimes when I was talking to Professor Blake."

"A human can get turned into a werewolf from an attack."

"And, was Conner?"

"No. The attack was too bad. Conner was dead."

"So you were just there for a day and left?"

"No. I was there for three days."

"Why three days?"

Professor Blake sighed. "This is the type of thing you would learn in class. But I'm going to answer it for you. Essentially, werewolves are active for three days a month. Not one."

"What three days?"

"The day before the full moon, the day of the full moon and the day after the full moon."

"See! That is just like Buffy," I exclaimed.

"You need to stop doing that," Blake admonished.

"Fine," I grumbled. "So why were you there three days?"

"I was hunting." Blake's response was simple.

"You were hunting the werewolf?"

"Yes."

"Did you find it?"

"No."

"Would you have killed it if you found it?"

"Yes."

"Even though a werewolf is still human?"

"It's still a monster that kills."

"Do all of them kill?"

"What do you mean?" Professor Blake looked confused.

"Nothing," I said a little too hastily.

Professor Blake didn't look like he believed me, but he let it go. "I think it's important for you to at least give us a chance," he finally said.

I sighed resolutely. I knew I wouldn't get the answers I was looking for unless I at least pretended to be a part of Blake's cause.

"I'll go to a class," I sighed. "Just one to start."

Professor Blake smiled at my acquiescence. "Good."

I got to my feet. "Just one class for now. I can't promise anything."

"It's a start."

"The start of what?"

"Your future."

I couldn't help but think that Professor Blake's vision of my future was vastly different from my own.

22 TWENTY-TWO

When I left Professor Blake's office, I made my way over to the UC to meet Paris for coffee. I looked around the cafeteria, but didn't see her. I got my café mocha and sat down at an empty table to think. Unfortunately, I didn't get the alone time I so desperately needed.

"Did you stay after class to talk to Professor Blake?"

I looked up to see Matilda sliding into the chair across from me. She had her own coffee. Great.

"Yeah. I just wanted to ask him about the assignment," I mumbled.

"He is so cute."

"Hmm." Why wouldn't she just go away? Instead, she kept chatting aimlessly. I watched her tuck her curly brown hair behind her ear as she flirted with a group of guys at a table across the aisle. At least she could multi-task – irritate me, entice them. Two birds, one stone.

"You don't think he's cute?"

"He's a professor. He's not my type."

"He's everybody's type."

"Not mine."

"You have a boyfriend, right?"

I wasn't so sure I did anymore, but I didn't want to start sharing with Matilda. I had a feeling if I started she would spread my personal business all over the dorms before the night was out. "Yes."

"He's in Alpha Chi, right?"

"Yeah."

"All those guys are so cute and so ... just yummy."

"I haven't really noticed," I admitted.

"How could you not?"

"I guess I'm just more into my boyfriend than the others." A brief flash of Aric pushed into my mind. I pushed it right back out.

"That makes sense," Matilda didn't seem to notice my lack of interest in the conversation. "Is he hot?"

"I wouldn't be sleeping with him if I didn't think he was hot." That was the truth.

Matilda giggled. "I bet he's hot."

I chatted with Matilda for another twenty minutes before excusing myself. "I have to run to the book store." I had given up waiting for Paris, and I desperately needed to get away from Matilda before I started screaming at her to shut up.

"I'll go with you."

Great. I got up from the table, tossed my empty coffee cup into the garbage and walked down the hallway to the bookstore. Matilda was babbling about something, but I was tuning her out. I could care less what Rick No. 1 smelled like.

When we got to the bookstore, I separated quickly from Matilda. She was distracted by a group of guys by the magazine rack anyway. I could only hope I'd be able to get my supplies and exit without her rediscovering me.

I wandered up and down the aisles for a few minutes until I found a stack of blue books. I needed them for my English classes. I was deciding how many to purchase when I felt a presence behind me. For a second, I thought that Matilda had found me again. The presence behind me was decidedly male, though. I swung around to smack into Aric's broad chest. This was getting to be an everyday occurrence – not that I minded.

"We need to stop running into each other like this," I muttered.

Aric chuckled throatily, almost like a growl. "I don't mind."

"I bet."

Aric ran his hand through his dark black hair to push his bangs out of his face. He looked down at me appraisingly. "Buying blue books?"

"Nothing gets past you."

"Are you always this ... verbally aggressive?"

"I'm aggressive physically, too." Whoops. That came out wrong.

Aric's already dark eyes went even darker as he regarded me. "I'll have to take your word for that. For now."

I didn't know how to take the statement so I decided to ignore it. "What are you here for?"

"Just to browse."

My eyes narrowed dangerously. "Are you following me?"

"Why would I be following you?"

There was no answer to the statement that wouldn't make me seem full of myself, I realized. I might as well let him think I was full of myself, I figured. "Maybe you think I'm hot."

"Maybe," Aric agreed.

"I keep running into you."

"Just lucky I guess."

I decided to change my approach. "You're fraternity brothers with my boyfriend."

"Is that a question?"

"Just an observation."

"Yes. I know Will." I could see the hint of distaste that flashed over Aric's face. It was gone as quickly as it was there, though.

"You don't like him?"

"I don't spend a lot of time with him."

"Why not?"

"I don't know."

"You don't know?"

"I don't spend a lot of time with any of them."

"But you live at the frat house."

"No, I don't."

That took me by surprise. "I saw you there."

"I said I didn't live there. I didn't say I never went there."

"You were there in the morning."

"Keeping tabs on me?" Aric couldn't hide his smile – or his dimples. What is it with weird guys and to die for dimples anyway?

"If you don't live there, why were you there so early in the morning?"

"I had to pick up a book I left there the night before." Aric didn't stumble across the answer, but I still knew it was a lie.

"You should be more organized."

Aric smirked. "Are you organized?"

"We weren't talking about me."

"What were we talking about?" I felt my skin sort of hum as Aric leaned in slightly. "Let's talk some more about you?"

"Let's talk about you," I tried to shift so I wasn't so close to Aric. He wasn't exactly making that possible.

"What do you want to talk about me for? I'm boring."

No one that looked like him could be boring, I thought. As if he was reading my mind, Aric smiled warmly.

"Why don't you like Will?" I was trying to catch Aric off guard.

"I just don't have a lot in common with him."

"You're fraternity brothers with him," I pointed out.

"That doesn't really mean anything. Do you have things in common with your roommates?"

"Yes." Well, Paris at least.

"Even that uptight little blonde one?"

He had me there. "No, but I didn't choose to live with her. I just got placed with her."

"Well, I didn't choose Will either."

"What did he do to you?"

"What makes you think he did anything to me?"

"You have to dislike him for a reason."

"He's cocky."

"And you're not?"

Aric smiled again. "Maybe. I can back it up, though."

I definitely didn't want to go there. "You dislike him because he's cocky?"

Aric ignored the question. "How long have you been with him?"

"On and off for four years."

Aric looked surprised. "You were with him last year?"

I knew what Aric was thinking – and I was irritated. "We weren't exclusive. When he went away to school we figured it would be easier to have an open relationship." I wasn't sure why I felt the need to defend Will to him.

"You don't strike me as an open relationship type of girl."

"You don't know anything about me."

"I know more than you think."

"What's that supposed to mean?"

Aric shrugged and finally backed up to let me get some air. I felt relief -- and a weird sense of loss at the same time. What the hell is wrong with me?

"I don't know you very well, you're right," Aric said. "I do know one thing, though."

"And what's that?"

"You need to be careful."

"What do you mean? You're the third person to tell me that in the past two days and I'm a little sick of hearing it."

Aric looked surprised. "Who else told you that? Will?"

I hadn't talked to Will in days, but I didn't want to give Aric any information he could use over me. "No, not Will."

"Who then?"

"No one."

Aric grimaced when he realized I wasn't going to tell him what he wanted to know. "Just be careful."

Aric then turned his back with what looked like a clear purpose. I didn't know what that purpose was, but all the men in my life – whether I wanted them to be in my life or not – were acting extremely weird lately -- and I was sick of it.

23 TWENTY-THREE

After leaving the UC, I headed back toward the dorms. I was a little irritated that Paris had stood me up – but I figured she had a good reason. It wasn't like her to just forget me or maybe that was my ego talking.

When I got to the room, Paris was sitting on the couch watching General Hospital.

"Where were you?"

Paris looked confused.

"Coffee?"

"Oh, God, I forgot. I'm sorry." So much for being unforgettable.

I didn't have the energy to even feign indignant anger. "It's fine."

I sat down on the couch and watched the rest of the soap with Paris. After that we decided to go to an early dinner.

"I have a lot of homework to do tonight," she explained.

I didn't, but I was hungry. We made our way down to the cafeteria. I was happy that it was potato bar night. It's the little things that calm you sometimes. As a food lover, there was nothing that bacon and cheese couldn't fix, especially when it was dumped on top of a hot baked potato.

We sat with a few guys from our floor – including Rick No. 1. He greeted us warmly. We kept the conversation light. That was a good thing since my mind was so busy.

"I'm thinking of joining Alpha Chi," Rick No. 1 admitted.

This took me by surprise. He didn't strike me as a fraternity guy. "Why?"

He shrugged. "I don't know. They just seem like a lot of fun."

I refrained from letting my true feelings be known. I didn't know how he would take the fact that I was starting to think they might be a frat full of sociopaths and date rapists.

After dinner, we returned to our room. Paris sat down and started writing a paper on her laptop. I turned the television on. I wasn't really watching anything; I just wanted the noise.

After about an hour, my cellphone rang. I looked at it and saw that it was Will. I debated not answering for a minute, but then I decided that probably wasn't the way to go.

"What's up?"

"What's up with you?" I didn't know if I expected Will to act differently, but he wasn't.

"Nothing. Just watching television."

"You have homework to do?"

"No."

"You want to spend some quality time with the handsomest guy you know?"

I smiled despite myself. "What kind of quality time?"

"Just regular quality time."

I debated the thought internally. I just wasn't ready to let him go yet, I realized. "Sure."

"Can you be ready in twenty minutes?"

"Sure."

"I'll pick you up downstairs."

I hung up the phone. Paris was watching me with a raised eyebrow.

"Are you going to Will's?"

I averted her gaze. "Yeah."

"Have fun."

I was surprised by her response, but I pushed it out of my mind as I went into the bedroom to pack a bag.

Brittany and Tara were returning to the room as I was leaving.

"Where are you going?" Brittany seemed like she was in a good mood. I could only hope I would ruin it on my way out.

"To Will's."

Brittany frowned. "Why?"

"I thought we would have some dirty sex."

Brittany stiffened at my flippancy. "Well, have a good night."

"I will."

Mission accomplished.

When I went out to the parking lot, Will was waiting. I got in the car and was surprised when he greeted me with a warm kiss.

"What was that for?"

"Can't I miss you?"

"You missed me?" I smiled at him, feeling the first relief I'd felt all day.

"I always miss you. Don't you miss me?"

"Of course," I answered him automatically. The truth was, though, I wasn't sure if I had missed him.

Will did the majority of the talking over the five-minute ride to his house. If he noticed my silence, he didn't say anything about it.

When we got to his frat house, we both climbed out of the car. Will absentmindedly grabbed my bag. I was struck for a second by the fact that he had been part of my life for so long that I couldn't imagine what it would be like if he wasn't there anymore. I didn't want to think about that, though. Not tonight at least.

When we entered the fraternity house there was a large group of guys sitting in front of the television playing Call of Duty.

"Do they ever do anything else?"

Will shrugged. "Boys like toys."

I didn't think that was a significant answer, but I didn't feel like arguing so I let it go. Without realizing what I was doing, I scanned the room. I didn't want to admit that I was looking for Aric, but I was. I felt a little disappointed when I didn't see him. Then I mentally slapped myself for thinking that.

"Hi, Zoe."

I wasn't sure which one of the guys had greeted me, but I responded with a general hello to everyone in the room. None of them looked up, but everyone else uttered a variety of different greetings.

"Who's winning?"

No one answered me. I saw a figure enter the far side of the room. Before focusing on him, I knew it was Aric. He had a certain presence. I looked up and met his gaze. He was frowning at Will.

For his part, Will was studiously avoiding making eye contact with Aric. I decided to test Will.

"Who is he?" I asked in a low voice, but for some reason I felt the room go suddenly silent. Had they heard me?

"Just a fraternity brother," Will brushed off my question. "Let's go to my room."

I followed Will dubiously, casting one glance back at Aric. He wasn't looking at me, though. He was glaring at Will's back.

Once in Will's room, he popped in a movie and we lazed on the bed to watch it. It was a horror movie. One of the better ones I'd seen recently called *Cabin Fever*. The twists were pretty interesting. Plus, who doesn't love a kid with a mullet?

After the movie, Will was feeling amorous. Truthfully, I could use the release, too. I pushed any suspicions out of my mind. When we were done, Will drifted off to sleep. I wasn't as lucky.

Left alone with my thoughts, I couldn't help but run the last few days through my mind.

One would think that vampires being real would be my big worry. That wasn't my primary concern, though. I was more worked up about the fact that everyone kept warning me to be careful – like there was something special about me.

Finally, I drifted off. It was an uncomfortable sleep, though. And my dreams? They were filled with big teeth and rivers of blood. I woke with a start.

It was still dark in the room – which meant it wasn't morning yet. I laid still for a moment, trying to figure out what had woken me up.

Then I heard something. I couldn't identify it, though. It sounded almost like ... animals.

For a second, I thought I must still be dreaming. The noises continued, though.

I looked over at Will. Only Will wasn't there. His side of the bed was empty.

I got to my feet slowly. I checked to make sure I was dressed. I had put my shorts and T-shirt back on, thankfully, and I opened the door. I waited and listened some more. The sounds continued. They were upstairs. It sounded like they were torturing a dog.

I froze. I knew I shouldn't investigate. Still, the thought of an animal being in pain infuriated me. I quietly ascended the stairs. I looked around, but there was no one milling about in the stairway -- below me or the room above me.

As I climbed, another thought entered my mind. What if it wasn't a dog? What if it was a girl?

I sucked in my breath and entered the main living room on the other side of the stairwell.

I don't know what I was expecting. It certainly wasn't what I found.

24 TWENTY-FOUR

I crept close to the wall, plastering my hands flat against the hallway wall behind me. I could hear voices. Briefly I wondered how I could mistake human voices for animal noises, but I pushed on. That really wasn't what was important right now.

I slipped behind a door that was mostly closed, but still cracked open. I peered through the opening, taking care to keep myself hidden. What I saw left me flummoxed.

There were about fifty fraternity brothers in the room – including Will and Aric – and they were all situated in a large circle. It looked like a ritual of some sort. I just hoped they weren't doing some sort of human sacrifice.

There was one guy standing in the center of the room. He seemed to be the leader.

"We have to be careful," he said. "We need to make sure that we don't draw attention to ourselves."

"We are being careful," I wasn't sure who said that. It was someone in the crowd, though.

"I don't think you are. There are rumors."

"What rumors?"

"There was some sort of scene outside the library the other day with one of the girls."

Now this was getting interesting. I couldn't help but wonder if it had been the same scene I had not only witnessed – but also had gotten myself involved in.

"What happened?" Another voice from the masses.

"Some guy confronted his girlfriend about what she did here the other night." The leader again. "And he did it in front of a bunch of people at the library. Then some other girl got involved to the point that it drew an even bigger crowd."

The leader swung around until he was facing Will at this point. Will lowered his gaze. "And it was your girlfriend, Will."

Uh-oh.

Everyone in the room swiveled to look at Will, and I swear I heard a couple of growls.

"You need to control her," the leader continued.

"What do you mean?" Will swallowed hard.

"She is out of control."

"Just because she stepped in and stood up for a girl she was worried was going to get smacked around?"

Well, at least Will was standing up for me.

"It's not just that and you know it," the leader warned. I figured he must be the president of the fraternity or something.

"What do you mean?" This time, I recognized the voice. It was Aric.

"She's going to be a problem," the leader responded.

"What kind of problem, Brett?" Aric again. He looked suddenly aggressive. I guess the leader's name was Brett.

"Don't be an idiot, Aric. You know where she's from. She could be a real problem."

"She's just a girl," Will said. "She doesn't know anything about any of that."

"Can you be sure?"

"I've known her for four years. I think she would have told me."

"Does she tell you everything?" Aric was regarding Will suspiciously.

"She's not known for keeping her mouth shut." This was true.

"What is she known for?" Brett asked the question, but all the guys in the room snickered as they waited for the answer.

"She's off limits," Will warned. "She's my girlfriend. She has been for four years. Those are the rules."

"Only if she's not a threat," Brett warned. "The pack takes precedence over your love life."

The pack?

"I thought you guys had an open relationship?" Aric asked the question. If I could smack him right now, I would.

Will's eyes narrowed as he regarded Aric. Since Aric was a full eight inches taller than him, I had to give him credit for not cowering in fear.

"What do you mean?"

"I thought you had an open relationship when you were up here and she was still in high school." Aric was being super-aggressive right now and I couldn't figure out why.

For his part, Will wasn't backing down. "How could you know that?"

Don't say it. Please don't say it. I was mentally trying to broadcast my intentions to Aric. Of course, it didn't work.

"That's what she told me yesterday."

"She told you?" Will not only looked angry, but hurt as well, by Aric's admission.

I noticed that the rest of the frat guys seemed content to watch the show. No one was trying to step between the two men who were puffing up like squabbling tom cats.

"I ran into her at the UC."

"And she just volunteered that? That doesn't sound like Zoe." Will looked confused and angry. I felt a little guilty. "You met her and she just told you that after five minutes?"

Aric smirked. "It wasn't the first time we've met. In fact, I've run into her a couple of times."

I mentally cursed Aric and his killer dimples. I thought I'd swore under my breath, but when I looked back up every set of eyes in the room was turned in the direction of my hiding place. Well, shit.

One of the fraternity brothers – I think his name was Craig – strode over and threw the door open, revealing me in my all my night-time wonder. Bedhead and all.

I tried to muster any courage I had – but given the situation I was in, I didn't exactly think I could muster much righteous indignation.

Craig grabbed my arm roughly and dragged me into the room – right in the center of the circle. I fought him angrily as the circle closed back around me. This wasn't good.

"Let me go!"

"What are you doing?" Will seemed concerned.

I tried to smooth my flyaway hair down. I noticed Aric's smirk as he saw my actions. "I woke up and you weren't there. I got concerned."

"Go back to bed," Will whispered. "I'll be there in a few minutes."

I'm not someone that follows orders, but I figured that was the most prudent move at this point. I was woefully outnumbered. I started to move back toward the crowd – but Will's fraternity brothers weren't moving.

"I don't think that's a good idea," Brett answered.

I swung around angrily. "And why is that?"

"You were listening at the door."

"I wasn't listening," I lied.

"Then why were you hiding behind the door?"

"When I realized you guys were having a meeting I wanted to hide because I didn't want anyone to see my bedhead." That's not entirely a lie. I drool on my hair in my sleep. It's not pretty. I figured I'd rather embarrass myself than tell the truth.

"Is that how you always look when you wake up?" Aric was looking me up and down.

I glared at him out of the corner of my eye. "You have a problem with that?"

"No. I love that you're not wearing a bra."

Will stepped forward and grabbed my arm, drawing me to his side and away from Aric. It was a territorial move and it momentarily made me forget that all of the fraternity brothers were now staring at my nipples through my thin tank top.

"What are you doing?" I seethed at Will.

"Protecting you."

Yep. That was my breaking point.

I dragged my arm away from Will angrily. "I don't need protection."

"Honey, that is exactly what you need at this point." Brett was looking smug.

"Listen, Captain Obnoxious, I'm not afraid of you." Sometimes my mouth works faster than my brain. I strode toward Brett and poked my index finger into the center of his chest. "I don't care how important you think being in this frat makes you. And, quite frankly, all it makes you look is so desperate you have to buy friends." Nothing could stop me now. "You need to grow up and realize the world doesn't revolve around you. You're not special. You're just a guy that gets his self-worth because he's in the hot frat." I made air quotes around hot. I gesture a lot when I'm worked up. "You're not special. You're just pathetic."

This time I wasn't mistaken, they were growling. What the hell?

I turned back and looked at Will. I wasn't feeling anything but disdain for him at the present moment. "I expected better from you."

Brett grabbed my arm roughly. "Maybe no one ever told you this – but women are to be seen and not heard in my house," he threatened.

"Then I'll just leave."

I tried to pull my arm away from Brett but he wasn't letting go. If anything, he was tightening his grip.

"Let me go!"

"No."

"Is this how you get your kicks? You threaten women into submission? And, when that doesn't work, you drug them and gang bang them?" I'd definitely gone too far. Brett was practically cutting off circulation at this point.

"We don't drug people," he seethed.

"You're so full of shit you smell like a dirty diaper."

Will gasped. I saw him take a step back and try to meld with his other fraternity brothers. I was way beyond my limit at this point. "You're a pussy. You know that? You used to be a rebel. You used to be fun. You used to be your own person. Now you're like a Borg with these morons."

I shoved hard against Brett's chest. He still didn't let go. "If you don't let me go, you're going to be sorry."

Brett smiled down at me disdainfully. "What are you going to do? Pull my hair?"

I smiled sweetly back. I was going to pull something. It just wasn't his hair. Without even realizing what I was doing I used my free right hand and rammed it hard into Brett's groin, grabbing a handful (and I'm being generous) of his most treasured possession and twisting.

For his part, Brett let go of my arm. He screamed in agony and fell to the floor grabbing his crotch as he twisted into the fetal position.

I rubbed my wrist. It was going to bruise later. I could tell.

I looked up at the room full of angry fraternity brothers. They looked like they wanted to rip me apart, but they didn't encroach on the circle.

Aric seemed to sense the hostility in the room. He grabbed my arm and started maneuvering me toward the front door. "You need to go," he warned.

"Yeah, I figured that out twenty minutes ago."

"Where's your stuff? In Will's room?"

"Yeah."

"Go get it," Aric shot a look around at his angry frat brothers. "And make it quick."

I nodded. I didn't feel like getting bossed around – but I desperately needed to get out of this house.

I threw my stuff together quickly, tossing on my jeans and hoodie. I dropped my bag at Aric's feet at the top of the stairs and zipped up the hoodie. "Thanks."

Aric smiled down at me. "For what?"

"For not being a sheep."

"No one here is a sheep."

"Well, they're not men either."

Aric regarded me for a second. "No, they're definitely not men."

As we moved toward the front of the door I stopped and swung around. I searched the crowd for Will. When my eyes met his, all I felt was pity. "Lose my number."

Will swallowed hard but he didn't answer me. "My home number, too. You are so not who I thought you were."

Aric gripped my arm and walked me out. He shot a parting glance at Will, too. I could only describe it as triumph.

25 TWENTY-FIVE

"**W**hat was all that about?"

Once we were outside and I could breathe again, I found my anger returning in a huge wave. It was a tsunami.

"Not here."

Aric directed me down the street. As we turned onto the next street, I saw him shoot a look back at the fraternity house. He watched it until it fell out of sight.

"Are you worried they are going to follow us?"

"No. They won't do anything that Brett doesn't order and he's probably still rolling on the floor in agonizing pain."

"He deserved it."

Aric smiled down at me. I couldn't help but notice how – in the moonlight – his eyes looked almost black instead of brown. "He definitely deserved it."

We fell into an amiable silence. It seemed to be a quiet agreement that he would be walking me all the way back to the dorms. I didn't mind. I didn't feel like being alone right now.

"So, what was that?"

Aric seemed to be struggling for an answer. "What do you think it was?"

That was the question, wasn't it? I decided to go for broke.

"Brett said it was a pack meeting. Is that like a wolf pack?"

Aric didn't answer.

"Or, maybe, a werewolf pack?"

Aric paused for a second and looked at me. "Why would you think that?"

"It has been a weird couple of days."

"You believe in werewolves?"

"I don't know," I answered honestly. "I staked a guy the other day and he turned to ash, so I believe in vampires." I laughed at myself for a second. "Now there's a sentence I never thought I'd utter."

Aric wasn't smiling. "You staked a vampire?"

"Yeah, he jumped me outside the dorms."

"How did you know to stake him?"

"It was just instinct." And seven seasons of *Buffy the Vampire Slayer*.

Aric mulled my story over for a few minutes. "Alright. What do you know?"

I realized that Aric wasn't going to share unless I did. I figured I owed him after he extricated me from the frat house. Plus, I was dying to tell someone. Why not an Adonis with great dimples?

I launched into the whole story – well, at least most of the story. For some reason I left out the parts about Rafael. I did tell him about Professor Blake and the training facility at the activities center, though.

Aric didn't seem surprised. "Yeah, we've known about the training facility for years."

"We?"

"The supernatural population."

"Which you're a member of?"

Aric turned and regarded me seriously. "I'm a werewolf."

I should have been stunned, but I wasn't. "So, were you bitten?"

"It's not always like that – no matter what that tool Blake told you."

"So, you weren't bitten?"

"My parents are werewolves – so I was born a wolf."

"So that whole biting people and turning them is a myth?"

"No. That's true. They're not true wolves, though. They're more like half wolves."

"What's the difference?"

"Real wolves have more power. We're strong. We can control the change."

"You mean you don't have to turn into a big hairy beast?"

Aric barked out a short laugh. "Basically."

I was curious – and Aric seemed to be in an answering mood – so I pressed on. "Do you only change on the three days around the full moon?"

"Seems like Professor Blake has been imparting some wisdom on you."

I waited for him to continue.

"Bit wolves can only turn on the three days of the full moon," he supplied.

"And born wolves?"

"We can change whenever we want to."

That was interesting. "What's it like?"

"What's what like?"

"When you change? What's it like?"

"It's painful."

"I bet. That's not what I mean, though. I've seen Silver Bullet, that can't be good. I mean, do you have any sense of you when you change?"

"Like can I think? Or do I just want to eat you?"

"Basically."

"We still know who we are when we change. Our emotions are stronger in wolf form – but we can control them," Aric stopped and looked down at me with a lazy smile. "That doesn't mean I still don't want to eat you."

I felt a thrill rush through me. That was probably a little inappropriate, though, since I'd just dumped my boyfriend of four years less than five minutes ago.

"Do you think now is the time to flirt?"

Aric didn't look chastised, but he did start walking again.

I decided to keep the conversation going and not dwell on the sudden urge I had to rip Aric's clothes off. "Is everyone in the frat a werewolf?"

"Not necessarily at the beginning. But they only let people in that are willing to turn."

"So Will is a werewolf?"

"Since last year, yeah."

How could I not notice that? Aric must have read my mind. "Unless you were around him on the days of the full moon you probably wouldn't have noticed."

I tried to think back – but honestly I never paid any attention to the moon phases.

"Don't you live in an area that is overpopulated with werewolves?" Aric looked curious.

"So I've been told. Either I'm really unobservant or I was really overprotected."

Aric smirked despite himself. "Well, you know now."

"Yeah, and I'm so thankful for that," I said sarcastically.

"Knowledge is always better than ignorance."

"Are you a fortune cookie now?"

"I'm a lot of things."

"Why are you part of the fraternity? Do you have to be?"

"When I first came here, I thought it would be great to be around a bunch of other wolves," Aric admitted.

"It wasn't?"

"Let's just say it wasn't what I was expecting."

"What do you mean?"

"My dad had always warned me that if you become a member of a pack that things are ... different."

"Different how?"

Aric sighed and motioned for me to sit on a bench. I realized we had made it to the center of campus. I sat down and looked at him expectantly.

"Sometimes, when wolves get together, there is an alpha vibe," he explained. "The longer they're together, the more time they spend together, the more they seem to think that they're somehow better than everyone else."

"I would have never thought that about Will," I admitted.

"He wasn't always like this?"

"No."

"What was he like?"

"He was a fun guy. We hung around. Got in trouble. Smoked a little pot. Heck, this past summer his mom didn't even live in the house. She lived in the backyard with some guy from the reservation."

"Which reservation?"

"I don't know. One of the ones north of Traverse City."

"That's a wolf reservation."

"Really?"

"Yeah."

"Will never mentioned it."

"He wouldn't. We're not supposed to tell anyone."

"You told me," I pointed out.

"Yeah, well, I'm not very good at following the rules."

I laughed despite myself. "I can see that."

"If you hate the pack, then why do you stay in the frat?"

"To make sure I am aware of what they are doing."

Aric's answer surprised me. "Did you know they were drugging girls?"

"You have proof of that?"

I told him about Brittany – and the girl at the library. He looked intense as he listened to me. "I have had my suspicions – but I could never prove anything."

"You suspected women were getting taken advantage of and you never did anything about it?" I was suddenly thinking he wasn't as good looking as I originally thought.

"This is a new thing," Aric explained. "They don't tell me anything. They don't trust me because I don't follow their doctrine."

I nodded like I understood – but I wasn't sure if I honestly did.

"We need to tell someone."

"Who?"

"Professor Blake?"

Aric seemed to consider the idea. "What are you going to tell him?"

"You mean, am I going to tell him about you?"

Aric flashed his dimples. "Maybe."

"I won't tell him about you. I just want to see if there's something he can do about the druggings."

"It's up to you."

"I'll think about it," I finally offered.

"All I ask is that you don't tell him without telling me you're going to do it."

I agreed and we set off walking toward the dorm again. When we got there, Aric offered to walk me up to my room.

"That's okay, I don't want to have to explain what happened right now. I need to think of a lie to tell them."

Aric nodded briefly. "I think you can trust Paris."

This surprised me. "You don't know her."

"She has a good vibe."

I laughed. "A good vibe? What's my vibe say?"

Aric moved a little closer to me. "Your vibe is X-rated."

"You're cute," I said as I took a step back. "I'm not ready to get X-rated with you, though."

"Why? You've already had sex with a wolf?"

"Yeah, and I just broke up with that wolf a half an hour ago."

"So, you're saying you need more time?"

"I need to think."

"I can understand that."

"Good. I'm not promising anything," I cautioned.

"I can wait." Aric's smile was decidedly wolfish at this point. "In fact, I bet I can wait longer than you."

That sounded like a challenge.

26 TWENTY-SIX

The next morning, I went to breakfast with Paris. She was surprised to find me in my bunk that morning, but she hadn't said anything in front of Brittany and Tara. Alone at breakfast, though, it was a completely different story.

"What happened?"

"We broke up."

"Why?"

"We just got into a fight and I realized it was over." That wasn't completely a lie.

"I'm sorry."

"It was bound to happen."

Paris was quiet for a few minutes. "I'm going to break up with Mike, too," she finally said.

"I know."

"Soon."

I regarded her briefly but didn't say anything else. There really was nothing to say.

Since it was Thursday, I only had two classes. After my classes, though, I had agreed to meet Professor Blake at the athletics center.

At 2 p.m. I found myself being ushered into the secret area by Blake. He was all business today, which was fine; I wasn't in the mood to annoy him right now. I didn't have the energy.

Blake took me to the library, where stacks of papers were sitting in the center of the table.

"What's this?"

"We just want to see where you're at."

"It's a test?" My eyebrows practically shot off my head. "You want me to take a test?"

"Yes."

"Good grief."

I had agreed to give this a shot so I sat down and started perusing the questions. I was surprised that it was more like an IQ test than anything else. There were no questions about the paranormal.

I hurried through the test. I really didn't care how I scored. I handed it to Blake and he seemed surprised by how quickly I'd completed it. He sat down to grade it – the irony wasn't lost on me – and then he got to his feet.

"Let's go to the training room."

"That's it? You're not going to tell me what my grade is?"

"It's not for a grade."

"Then what's it for?"

"My edification."

Cripes.

We walked down to the hall and into the training room. I was surprised to see two students waiting for us. They were both big, burly guys with necks that were as wide as their heads.

"Is this the steroid duo?"

"This is Rex and Don."

Rex? As in T-Rex? I decided not to voice that thought. I figured it would just enrage him.

"So what are we doing here?"

"Checking your reflexes." I was wrong; Blake did have a sense of humor. It was a sick one.

"Against them?"

"Yes."

"They're twice my size."

"And a vampire has three times the strength of a human, and you managed to kill one of them."

Rex looked surprised. "She killed a vampire?"

Professor Blake nodded.

"By herself?"

Blake nodded again.

For their part, Rex and Don were now eying me a little differently. That would only last until I started pulling their hair and screaming as a defense mechanism, I figured.

"And why are you checking my reflexes?"

"To make sure you have the physical ability to fight supernaturals." Professor Blake said it like it was the most normal thing. I had to fight the urge to giggle.

"Fine," I said resolutely. Maybe if they kicked my ass Blake would leave me alone?

I dropped my bag and moved to the center of the mats. "Let's do this," I said grimly.

Professor Blake looked nonplussed. "Don't you want to change your clothes?"

I looked down at my ripped jeans, Star Wars shirt and DC Comics high tops. "Why?"

Blake merely shook his head. "Fine."

I turned and looked at Rex and Don expectantly. "Come and get me boys."

Rex stepped up on the mats first. He started to circle me. I kept him in my gaze, but barely moved. What a tool. I bet he fancied himself on big time wrestling.

"I'll try not to hurt you too bad," Rex said with what I'm sure he thought was a reassuring smile.

"I'll try not to vomit on you," I offered.

Rex frowned. I couldn't figure out how he passed the IQ test.

While I was wondering, Rex took the opportunity to lunge at me. I saw it coming a mile away and side-stepped him.

Rex turned around, surprised. He lunged again. This time, I tripped him.

He hit the mats hard. While he was down, I quickly leaned into him with my knee and grabbed his left hand, applying pressure to the joint between his thumb and the rest of his hand. It was a trick I'd learned from my cousin years before.

Rex howled in pain. He tried to buck me off, but I had the leverage. "Tell me I'm the best," I goaded him.

I noticed that Don had stepped onto the mat. Well, this should be interesting. As he started making his way toward me, I considered what I should do. If I let go of Rex, I would be woefully outnumbered. If I didn't, there was only one thing to do -- and it was a pretty dirty move. Of course, we were fighting vampires here, so I didn't think it mattered how you won. Just that you won.

As Don descended on me, I made the decision. I reared my head back and slammed my forehead into his groin. When I made contact I was thankful that he wasn't wearing a cup. I figured neither of them felt they needed one since they were fighting a lowly girl. They wouldn't make that mistake again.

Don reared back and fell to the ground, moaning as he grabbed his nuts. Three times in one week, I was on a roll.

"Enough!"

Blake made his way onto the mats and pulled me off of Rex. Rex rolled over and glared at me. Since Blake was there, though, he didn't make a move.

"That was cheating," Don gasped.

"And two huge guys fighting one little girl isn't?"

Blake regarded me with his light eyes for a second. I couldn't read his mind, but I think he was impressed.

Blake dismissed both Rex and Don. The two boys glared at me as I left. I had a feeling their egos were bruised – just like Don's nuts.

After they left, Blake walked toward the refrigerator in the back of the room and pulled out a bottle of water. He handed it to me – still not saying anything.

"So, did I pass?"

"Yes."

"Great. Now what?"

"Where did you learn to fight like that?"

"I hung around with more boys than girls growing up."

"And?"

"And boys like to wrestle. Even after I started getting boobs they wanted to wrestle – but I think it was so they could feel me up."

Blake ignored my inappropriate sexual humor. "Your reflexes are off the charts. As was your written test."

"That was an IQ test."

"It wasn't really an IQ test. It was just to test your mental acuity."

"So my mental acuity is fine?" Whatever that means.

"Your mental acuity is fine – at least as far as that test."

"Cool. I'm a genius."

"You're special. You're not a genius."

"Special? Like Rain Man special or ride the short bus special?"

Blake sighed. I forgot he hated my pop culture references. Okay, maybe I didn't forget.

"No one has ever tested as high as you."

"Great, another item for my resume. I'll list it right after Photoshop and right before National Honor Society."

"You didn't put any effort into either, though," he mused.

"I'm gifted, what can I say?"

"I think it has more to do with genetics."

"What does that mean?"

"What do your parents do?"

"My mom is in real estate and my dad is a contractor."

"They have no special abilities?"

"Unless you count embarrassing me, then no."

Professor Blake didn't look like he believed me.

"I'm not lying. They're just regular people."

"You're not a regular person."

"That's what I tell everyone. They just don't believe me."

Professor Blake just shook his head as he left the room. I guess the conversation was over.

27 TWENTY-SEVEN

After leaving Professor Blake's wacky monster mashing academy, I decided I needed some clarification. I would have to call my parents.

There was just too much chatter about home and pedigrees and werewolves instead of dog men. It was just too much.

Thankfully, when I got back to my dorm room, none of my room-mates were there. I needed complete privacy for what I was about to do. If anyone overheard – especially Brittany – campus mental services would be banging on the door faster than Don fell to the ground massaging his nuts.

I pulled out my cellphone and punched in my home number. My mother picked up on the third ring.

"Oh, hi, honey. Glad to you finally decided to call home."

"It's been a busy week, Mom."

"Too busy for you to call the woman who gave birth to you?"

"It was a busy week," I repeated.

"Twenty-four hours of agony, and let me tell you, little missy, your head was so big it almost killed me when it passed."

When my mom gets started, it's just best to let her go. She can guilt trip with the best of them. After about five minutes of this, she finally fell silent.

"How are things at home?"

This set her off again. "Your aunts are crazy."

What else was new?

"Your cousins are in trouble."

What else was new?

"We're having a family Halloween in a couple weeks."

"Together?"

"Yes."

"I thought you were all fighting?"

"We'll have made up by then."

What else was new?

I kept up the inane chitchat with my mother while I decided how best to approach the subject. How do you ask your mom about werewolves and vampires?

The conversation went on a full half an hour and I still couldn't find an opening – or the courage – to ask the questions I needed to know. Finally, I realized it just wasn't going to happen, so I finally said goodbye and disconnected – but not before promising I would consider coming home for the Halloween holiday. What? I said I would consider it. I didn't say I would actually do it.

The next day I went to all three of my classes and – thankfully – nothing out of the ordinary happened. I didn't bother stopping to talk to Professor Blake as I left. It was Friday. I was looking forward to a weekend without monsters.

When I got back to the dorms, I watched *General Hospital* with Paris. Sadly, I was becoming as addicted as she was. If Sam and John didn't get their happily ever after, I was going to be furious.

"They were on another show together," Paris explained.

"Who?"

"Kelly Monaco and Michael Easton."

"Who?"

"The actors who play John and Sam."

"Oh. What show?"

"It was called *Port Charles* and John was an evil vampire and Sam was his evil love interest."

"They had a soap about vampires?"

"Yeah. It was great."

I bet.

We waited for Tara and Brittany before we went down to dinner. After the blowup a couple of nights before, things had settled down. They were still tense –but not uncomfortably tense.

During dinner, Brittany chatted away happily. She was doing great in her classes – and there was some guy in biology that apparently wanted to check out her biology. I could only hope that would happen.

"So, what are we doing tonight?"

I turned to Brittany in surprise. "You want to go out with us?"

"Yeah," she said enthusiastically. "As long as we're not going to one of Will's fraternity parties."

"I don't think you have to worry about that anymore."

"Why?"

"Will and I broke up," I admitted.

"On, no," Brittany seemed genuinely sad for me. "Do you want to have a girls' night in? We can watch *Pretty Woman* or something. We can paint our toe nails and put on mud masks and just hang out until you feel better."

That sounded like hell.

"Mike is having a party," Paris offered.

I looked at her in surprise. "You want to go?"

Paris nodded. "I think it would be a good idea. He's been bugging me to go, and with you guys there, I won't have to stay."

"Why wouldn't you want to stay?" Tara asked.

"I don't know," Paris shrugged. "He's just irritating me."

Tara let it go and we spent the rest of dinner listening to Brittany excitedly plan for the party. "What do you think I should wear?"

"Something slutty," I offered.

Brittany slid a glare my way. "I'm going to let that go. I've decided you think you're being funny and you're not."

I decided to let that go. I was in the mood to go out and I didn't feel like starting World War III beforehand.

After dinner, we took turns showering. We let Brittany go first because we figured she would take the longest to get ready and the rest of us followed.

The weather was still decidedly warm, so I went with my simple jeans and hoodie ensemble. I put on my favorite Star Wars hoodie and paired it with my Joker DC Comics high-tops.

Paris' outfit looked a lot like mine. In fact, she asked if she could borrow my Wonder Woman low-tops.

When we walked out into the main room, I had to stifle a giggle when I saw Brittany. She had hot rollers in her hair and she was painting her nails. I didn't even know they still made hot rollers.

She frowned when she saw how Paris and I were dressed. "You're not getting dressed up?"

"Why would we?"

"To look nice. You're single now. You're not going to attract a man looking like that."

"I put out – that will always attract a man," I shot back.

Brittany pursed her lips and turned back to her fingernails.

It was another hour before we were ready to go. Brittany had decided on khaki pants and a button-down sweater. She looked like a kindergarten teacher. I figured that might turn some guys on, though, so I let it go.

We all walked together to Mike's. Tara and Brittany were a few feet ahead of Paris and me. She seemed nervous.

"Are you going to break up with him tonight?"

"I'm thinking about it."

"What's holding you back?"

"I don't want a big scene."

"Just wait until the end of the night."

"What? Hey, by the way, I want to breakup. Don't call me again. Goodbye."

"Sounds good to me." That was pretty much what I had done with Will, after all.

"What if he is so drunk he forgets?"

"Yeah, that could be a problem," I admitted.

"I think I'll just play it by ear."

When we got to the party, Mike practically mauled Paris when he saw her. I smirked as I moved past her. She shot me a dirty look.

Brittany and Tara already had their drinks and had found a group of guys to talk to in the corner. I filled my red cup with cheap keg beer. It wasn't great, but this was college, I figured I'd better get used to it. Apparently, you drink better in high school than college.

Paris found me about fifteen minutes later. She wasn't happy. "Thanks for abandoning me."

"Well, I wasn't about to join you in a threesome, so what else was I supposed to do?"

Paris slammed her cup of beer and glared at me. I figured if she did that two more times she would forget she was angry with me.

As she made her way back to the keg, I decided to hide out on the balcony until she was sufficiently soused. I'm not afraid of confrontation; I just didn't want it to kill the buzz I planned on having in an hour.

When I stepped outside I was struck by how cold it had suddenly gotten. Fall was definitely on the way. So much for Indian summer. I was a little bummed. I also wasn't alone. I noticed a dark figure on the far side regarding me. It was Rafael – and this was exactly the place I had met him two weeks ago. Briefly, I couldn't help but reflect that this had probably been the longest and most eventful two weeks of my entire life.

"What are you doing here? Looking for dinner?"

Rafael raised his eyebrows suggestively. "Why? Are you on the menu?"

I flushed. Luckily it was dark. What was it with guys and the suggestive eating comments lately?

"Where did you take off to the other night?"

"What do you mean?"

"You looked like you were on a mission."

"Just checking some things out."

"Like what?"

"Why are you so curious?"

"It's part of my nature."

"So I've noticed."

I decided to let that statement go. I was pretty sure he meant it as an insult. "So, did you find out who I killed?"

Rafael seemed surprised. "What makes you think I care?"

I furrowed my brow. "Don't you all hang out together?"

"No."

"Why not?"

"Do you hang out with all loud blondes?"

Well, that was rude – and probably spot on. "I didn't mean anything. I was just … ." There really was no graceful way out this so I changed tactics. "So you don't know who it was?"

"I have my suspicions."

I waited for him to continue. He didn't. "And who do you suspect?" I prodded.

Rafael looked uncomfortable. He clearly wasn't ready to share any information with me.

Luckily, the sound of the doors sliding open interrupted the uncomfortable atmosphere that had descended on the small balcony. Paris stepped out unsteadily. I saw her look from me to Rafael for a few seconds. Yep, things were even more uncomfortable now.

Rafael took advantage of the momentary distraction of Paris' arrival to excuse himself. He didn't say goodbye.

Once he was gone, Paris raised her eyes suggestively at me. "So, are you going to start sleeping with the vampire now?"

28 TWENTY-EIGHT

Because of the party, I didn't have a chance to question Paris about her vampire statement for the rest of the night. The next morning, we all had breakfast together. It was a constant conversation stream of Brittany going on and on about all the guys she claimed had hit on her the night before and me wanting to reach across the table and throttle her. I was about to explode.

After breakfast, I asked Paris if she wanted to go for a walk. I could only hope that Brittany and Tara wouldn't ask to be included. I needed some answers, and I needed them now.

Thankfully, Brittany and Tara said they were going back upstairs to study. When Paris and I left the building, I could barely contain myself.

"How did you know that Rafael was a vampire?"

Paris smiled. "It was pretty obvious."

"How? He's tan."

"That's just a myth."

"What is?"

"That vampires are all pale," she said. "They don't sparkle either."

"I figured that out myself."

"Vampires have a dark aura," Paris supplied. "They're dark red. Almost purple really."

"You see auras?"

"Yeah."

"How?"

Paris paused for a second and then turned to me seriously. "I have something to tell you. I just don't know how you're going to take it."

I was taken aback. Paris had a secret. Then again, who didn't have a secret these days?

"I'm a witch," she said simply.

So not what I was expecting. "A witch?"

"Well, a Wiccan to be more exact."

I was confused. "What's the difference?"

"Wiccans are nature-based witches," Paris explained.

"Are there other types of witches?"

Paris laughed. "There are a lot of different types of witches, just like there are a lot of different types of people."

This was the second time in less than twenty-four hours when someone had accused me of being bigoted. Maybe I should rethink my outlook?

"What type of witch are you? Do you do spells?"

Paris considered the question carefully. "Define spells."

"You know, spells."

"Like in Harry Potter?" Paris' eyes were sparkling.

I never realized how irritating that was. Now I understand why Professor Blake looked like he wanted to throw me through a wall whenever I did it.

"I know it's not like Harry Potter, I scoffed. "Is it like *Charmed*, though?"

"No, I don't have magical powers."

"Then what do you do?"

"It's a long story."

Paris explained her family history and, she was right, it was a long story.

"My whole family is what would loosely be considered Pagans," she started.

"You mean like animal sacrifices?"

"I suppose, back in the day, they did stuff like that. We don't though. Wiccans believe in karma. At least my family does. The primary Wiccan rule is to harm no one."

That is totally like *Charmed*. I didn't say it out loud, though. I was trying to refrain from making people think I watched too much television.

"So do you do spells?" She still hadn't answered the initial question.

"We do some spells," Paris said cautiously.

"What kind of spells?"

"Nothing major. Some protection spells. Some karma enhancements." I noticed Paris was avoiding all eye contact.

"What else?"

Paris sighed. "My family wasn't always so ... pure."

Now what did that mean? I let her continue.

"There were times when we didn't follow the Wiccan rules."

"What happened?"

Paris looked conflicted. "Not everyone in my family is good. Some of my relatives – not my parents or my brothers or sisters or anything – but some of my relatives are into the darker stuff."

I wanted more details, but I didn't want to push her too far. I decided that if I wanted Paris to open up completely to me, I was going to have to do the same with her. So I told her. I told her everything. I told her about Professor Blake and his monster academy. I told her about Will and Aric and the frat house full of werewolves. I told her about the vampire outside of the dorm rooms. I told her about Rafael and his cryptic warnings. When I was done, she looked stunned.

"Holy shit!"

That had been my initial reaction, too, so I let her process it for a few minutes.

"Why didn't you tell me any of this?"

"I didn't know what to say. I thought you would think I was crazy."

"Are you going to join the academy?"

"I don't know," I admitted. "It feels like I'm being pushed that way, but I'm not sure it's something I want to do. They seem to be of the mind that all supernaturals are bad and I just don't think they all are."

"You mean Aric and Rafael?"

"I'm pretty sure Aric is a good guy," I admitted.

"You're not as sure about Rafael, though?"

"He's more mysterious," I admitted.

"He's probably had to be."

I nodded. That made sense.

"Have you told Blake about Aric and Rafael?"

"No. Absolutely not."

"So, your first instinct was to protect them?" Paris mused.

"I guess. The truth is, I'm still not sure what they're doing at their little academy. They're clearly gearing up for some big fight – but I don't know what they're fighting against."

"Have you asked them?"

"Not really," I said.

"Why?"

"The truth is, I feel that if I ask them I'm going to find out things I don't want to know."

"Well, you went back so you must have some interest in what they're doing."

I hated it when someone confronted me with practical information. "Maybe I'm just curious."

Paris pursed her lips. She didn't look like she believed me. The problem was, I didn't know if I believed it either.

"Are you worried about the wolves?"

"What do you mean?"

"They're clearly threatened by you. And Aric is big, but I don't think he could fight off a whole wolf pack – no matter how badly he wants to get in your pants."

I hadn't really thought about it. The question made sense, though. I shrugged in response. "Wouldn't they have come after me already?"

"Maybe they're waiting to see what you do."

"I'm not planning to do anything."

"What do you think Professor Blake would do?"

"I'm not planning on telling him, so I'll never know."

"Do Aric and Rafael know about each other?"

"What do you mean?"

Paris must have read the confusion washing over my face because she stifled a smirk. "Not that they're both fighting for your affections. I'm talking about the fact that they both exist as, you know, super-naturals?"

"You mean he's a werewolf and he's a vampire?"

"Yes."

I hadn't really thought about it. "I don't know. Do you think I should tell them?"

Paris seriously considered the question. "I don't know. If history is any indication, I would say no."

"History?"

"Traditionally, werewolves and vampires don't get along?"

"Like *Twilight*, you know, fighting to the death?"

"I don't think *Twilight* should be used as the basis for anything – especially good storytelling – but I do think there is something to vampires and wolves fighting. My mom told me stories when I was a kid."

"There must be a reason?"

"Testosterone?"

"Are all vampires and wolves men?"

"No."

"Then it can't be testosterone."

"I guess not."

"It's probably just clan bullshit."

"Clan bullshit?"

"You know, both clans thinking they're superior."

"Probably."

"So what are you going to do?"

"I honestly don't know." I was getting sick of admitting that to myself.

"Well, you probably don't want to hear this, but until you decide you should probably try to stay away from all three of them," Paris suggested.

"All three of them?"

"Aric, Rafael and Professor Blake."

"I have class with Blake."

"Well, then don't talk to him after class."

It sounded like a good idea on paper. The problem was, I didn't know how practical a solution it would actually turn out to be in real life.

29 TWENTY-NINE

After telling Paris all my secrets, I felt relieved. The rest of the day flew by. At dinner that night, Brittany asked the inevitable question – well, inevitable for Brittany.

"So, what are we doing tonight?"

If Brittany was a 'we' person with her roommates, I would hate to see her when she finally got into a relationship.

"I want to dance," Paris finally said.

"We'll have to go to a bar for that." The idea wasn't thrilling to me.

"Better than a lame party with flat beer in red plastic cups," Paris replied.

She had a point.

"I don't want to go to some meat market," I countered.

"No, we'll go someplace small," Paris agreed.

"What's a meat market?" Brittany's innocent question made Paris snicker and me roll my eyes.

"You explain it to her," I told Tara as I walked into the bedroom.

Later that night we had all agreed to go to a local bar that was full of more townies than coeds, ironically called The Haunt.

"I hope they're talking about middle-aged drunks and not ghosts," I whispered to Paris during the walk to the dive.

Once we got there, I changed my opinion. "I hope it's middle-aged losers with beer guts instead of roaches."

Paris forced me in. Since we were under twenty-one, we had to deal with large black X's on our hands instead of the customary bar stamp. I wasn't in the mood to drink anyway. I wasn't actually in the mood to dance, either. Instead, I decided to play some pool.

I was a pretty good pool player – and I'm not just saying I was a pretty good pool player for a teenage girl. I had grown up with a pool table in my grandparents' basement. All of my cousins and I were pretty good.

After a friendly game with a couple of students, I noticed a guy watching me from the corner of the bar. He looked to be about thirty. I figured he had to be a loser to be hanging out at a bar on a college campus – but that wasn't going to stop me from taking his money in a friendly pool game.

We agreed to put ten dollars on it. I won – but I downplayed my ability. Of course, he asked for a rematch, upping the ante to twenty. I won again. By the third game, we were starting to draw a crowd. That was fine with me. All men think that women can't play pool. All men are willing to empty their wallets to prove that fact – even when it's not even remotely true. I figured a shopping spree was just what I needed.

After about two hours, I was up three hundred dollars and I had no shortage of people willing to play. Everyone wanted to be the individual to take the snarky blonde down. This was mid-Michigan, though, none of them were exactly pool sharks.

Paris found me in the middle of one game – and watched until I finished. "I didn't know you could play pool."

"I'm multi-talented."

"So I see. How much are you up?"

"I don't know." That wasn't true. I just didn't want to rub it in. Plus, I wasn't done fleecing the natives.

After another hour, and another couple hundred bucks, the stakes were getting high. I'd upped it to fifty dollars a game and I was on quite a roll. That's why I didn't notice when a familiar face had joined the crowd.

"You guys are never going to beat her."

I froze when I heard the voice. I swung around to find Will watching – a nervous grin playing at the corner of his mouth.

"How would you know?" The local I was playing wasn't happy. I only had two balls left to his six. It wasn't looking good for him.

"She's the best pool player I've ever met," Will said. "I stopped playing her when I was sixteen. My ego couldn't handle it."

As if on cue, I sank my final two balls with one split shot. Thanks to Will's conversation starter, no one else wanted to play me. The crowd that had gathered dispersed and it was only Will and me left.

"Thanks for ruining my chances to make some more money," I admonished him, pushing the last fifty bucks into my pocket.

He regarded the hefty bulge in my pants and laughed. "I think you already cleaned up for the night."

We lapsed into an uncomfortable silence. Will sipped from his drink and then offered it to me.

"No one is looking," he offered.

Like I was going to take a drink from anyone in his fraternity. I shook my head. "I'm fine."

Will was nervous, I could tell. He shifted uncomfortably from one foot to the other, pushing his hair from his eyes. "About the other night ... ."

I didn't think a bar was a good place to talk, but I had no intention of going outside with him alone either.

"Don't worry about it."

"No, I feel I need to explain."

"That's not necessary," I responded quickly. "I already know everything."

Will's brown eyes narrowed. For a second, he looked dangerous.

His gaze softened slightly after that, but he was still clearly on edge. "What did Aric tell you?"

"Aric didn't tell me anything," I lied. "I have another source of information."

"Who?" Will's breathing pattern had picked up.

"It doesn't matter."

Will relaxed all of a sudden. "You don't know anything. You're just pretending you do."

Well, fuck him. "I know you're a werewolf," I seethed.

Will was on edge again. He looked around nervously and stepped closer to me. "That's ridiculous." Will licked his lips. That was always his tell in poker.

"Really? It's ridiculous?"

"Yes," Will averted his eyes from mine.

"You're the worst liar ever."

Will didn't say anything for a long time. Finally, he raised his eyes to mine. There was no malice there, only sadness.

"What are you going to do?"

"I'm not going to do anything," I answered simply.

"You're not?" Will seemed surprised.

"Why would I?"

"I don't know, I just thought … ."

"You thought what? I would run around campus and tell everyone that you're a werewolf? That wouldn't hurt you. It would hurt me."

Will still seemed uncomfortable. I knew why.

"You can tell your fraternity brothers that their secret is safe," I said pointedly. "As long as they stop drugging women … ." Will started to interrupt and I put my hand up to stop him. "There's no use denying it. I know it's the truth. If you stop drugging women and you don't go around using coeds as chew toys, I'll forget what I know."

"I don't think Brett will go along with that," Will said truthfully.

"Then we're going to have a problem." There was no point in lying, Will knew me too well.

"What do you want me to do?" Will was practically pleading now. "I can't protect you from all of them."

"I don't need you to protect me," I was getting angry now. "I never needed you to protect me. Just ... my God, Will, what happened to you?"

Will shot me a glare. "Nothing happened to me. I'm still Will. I'm just stronger. I'm faster."

"You're clearly not any smarter." The remark came out a lot more bitter than I meant it to.

"You don't understand," Will said. "I was always popular. Everyone thought I was cool up there. Up at home. "

"I remember. I was there."

"When I came here, it was different," Will looked suddenly broken to me. I wondered when that had happened – and how I hadn't noticed. "I was just another student here. Nobody noticed me. Nobody cared."

"So you thought becoming a monster would help?"

"I'm not a monster!"

"What do you call a guy that sits around and watches as his frat brothers drug women? What do you call a guy that doesn't stand up for himself – or his girlfriend?"

Will looked embarrassed momentarily, but then he seemed to regain himself. "There's a hierarchy that has to be followed."

"There's always going to be a hierarchy in a pack, Will," I said. "You're never going to get to the top because there's always going to be someone ahead of you. You're just one of the sheep for them to control."

If I had been getting through to him, I wasn't anymore. Will pulled away when I reached out to touch his arm. "You don't under-stand any of this. I knew you wouldn't. That's why I didn't tell you."

"You're right," I said, swallowing hard and stepping back. "I don't understand any of this. I don't understand how the sweet boy I knew let this happen."

"Maybe you will someday." Will's voice was wistful.

'I'll never understand this," I said forcefully. "I'll never understand you doing this. You being so weak. You being ... someone I don't even recognize."

Will must have heard the finality in my voice. "I guess this is goodbye then."

"It is goodbye."

Will started to turn and walk away. He swung back. "I'll make sure they know you're not a threat."

With those words, Will was gone into the crowd. "Goodbye, Will."

Paris was at my side quickly. "What happened?"

"What?"

"I saw you talking to Will. What happened?"

"Nothing," I waved my hand. "We just came to an understanding. I told him as long as his fraternity stops drugging girls that I would keep his secret."

"Do you think he believed you?"

"I don't know." It was hard to admit, but it was the truth.

We found Brittany hanging all over some guy on the dance floor. It took a while, but we managed to disengage her. "I wasn't going to do anything," she said sheepishly.

After a full forty-five minutes of searching, we still couldn't find Tara, though. Finally, we all decided to go back to the dorms without her.

"Maybe she went back without us?" Brittany asked hopefully.

"Maybe."

"Maybe she met someone," Paris offered.

"Maybe"

"She would have told us, though," Brittany said quietly.

The thing is, of all of my new roommates, Tara was the one that was still an enigma. Part of me agreed with Brittany that she wouldn't have left without telling us. There was a niggling doubt in the back of my brain, though.

Paris must have read my mind.

"Maybe she is back at the room?"

I could tell she didn't believe it either.

30 THIRTY

When we got back to the dorms, Tara wasn't there. After a quick inspection, I came to the realization that she hadn't returned to the room. Absolutely nothing had changed. All her stuff was still in the closet. Her books were still on her desk. The ratty old stuffed rabbit she slept with was placed gently on her pillow.

Tara was not here, nor had she been here.

Brittany was starting to panic. "Should we call the police?"

"And tell them what? We misplaced our roommate at the bar?"

"What if she was kidnapped?"

"From a bar full of people? We would have seen that happen."

Even as I said the words, I wasn't sure I was right. Paris made the final decision.

"If we still haven't heard from her in the morning, we'll call the police."

Brittany reluctantly agreed.

My dreams that night were not merely active, but tortured. I dreamt that Tara was taken from The Haunt forcibly – by a fraternity full of hairy beasts. Her scream as they dragged her out the door was enough to chill me to the bone.

I woke up to loud knocking on the dorm door. "What the hell?"

Brittany was up like a shot, racing to the door. I sat up and looked down to where Tara's bed was. It obviously hadn't been slept in. I noticed Paris looking, too. This wasn't good.

We both climbed out of bed and made it into the next room as Brittany threw the door open. We were all surprised to see two police officers standing on the other side.

"Is this the room for Tara Thompson?"

"Yes, did you find her?" Brittany looked relieved. I had a bad feeling, though.

"May we come in?"

Brittany let the two officers in. I noticed they were city police and not campus police. That made things all the more ominous.

The officers came into the room. When they saw a few curious faces peering in from the hallway, they closed the door behind them. Well, that couldn't be good.

Brittany, Paris and I stood in a semi-circle waiting for the officers to continue.

"When was the last time you saw your roommate?"

"Last night," I answered. "We all went to The Haunt together. When it was time to leave we couldn't find her, though. We figured she came back here."

"She wasn't here, though?"

"No, she wasn't here."

"You didn't think to call us when you couldn't find her?"

"I wanted to," Brittany said accusingly. "They wouldn't let me though. They said I was overreacting."

It was good to know she was good in a crisis.

The older officer – he looked to be in his mid-forties – turned to me. "You didn't think it was strange that she just disappeared?"

"I've only known her for two weeks. I don't know her bar habits." I didn't like his accusatory tone.

198 AMANDA M. LEE

"Well, maybe you should have erred on the side of caution." I definitely didn't like his tone now.

"What exactly are you accusing me of?"

Paris stepped in smoothly. "Maybe you should just tell us what is going on."

The younger officer seemed to sense Paris' concern about the situation. "Your roommate was attacked last night."

He said it so matter-of-factly. Like he was telling us our class schedule had suddenly changed.

"Was she raped? Was she drugged?"

Will had been at the bar the night before. Maybe some of his frat brothers had been there, too. Just because I hadn't seen them, that didn't mean that they weren't there – hiding in the shadows.

"Why would you think she was drugged and raped?" It was Officer Obnoxious again.

Here was a sticky situation. I had just promised Will the night before that I would keep his secret. Still, something had obviously happened to Tara the night before. I decided to take things slowly. "I watch a lot of television."

Neither officer looked like they believed me. I didn't blame them.

"We're still waiting for toxicology results," the younger officer said.

"Is she in the hospital? Is she okay?" Brittany looked like she was ready to spring into action.

The officers looked at each other uncomfortably. I didn't like their unease. I had an awful feeling what they were about to tell us.

"She's not in the hospital."

Paris and I exchanged dark looks.

"Is she at the station?" Brittany either didn't grasp the situation – or she just didn't want to. Denial is a powerful thing.

The younger officer seemed to realize that Paris and I already knew what they were going to say. He also knew Brittany did not. "Why don't you sit down," he prodded her gently.

"Why would I need to sit down?" Her voice was shrill now. "Why don't they have to sit down?"

Paris turned to Brittany and put her hand on her shoulder. "Brittany ... I don't think they're here to tell us Tara is at the station."

"What do you mean?" Brittany's lower lip was quivering.

"She means that Tara is dead," I snapped.

That was it. Brittany started wailing and threw herself into the younger officer's arms. He looked uncomfortable as he tried to comfort her. He turned his pleading dark eyes to Paris and then me. When he saw the resolute look on my face, though, he must have realized he was on his own when it came to comforting her.

I turned to Officer Obnoxious unsteadily. Even though I knew she was dead, I was hoping – even if it was just for a second – that he would tell me I was wrong. He didn't.

"How did she die?" Paris' voice seemed like it was coming from a million miles away.

"We found her in the alley behind The Haunt," the officer said.

"She was just left in the alley?" That didn't make sense. Why didn't they take her back to the frat house?

"Yeah. She was left in the alley like garbage. I'm guessing you didn't look in the alley for your friend?"

Fuck this guy. "Why would I look in the alley?"

"Why would you just leave her?"

"She's an adult. I thought she might have left with a guy or something."

"Had she done that before?"

"No," I admitted grudgingly.

"How did she die?" Paris asked the question again. She was clearly in some sort of shock.

I turned to Officer Obnoxious again expectantly. Now he looked uncomfortable.

"We're not exactly sure."

"How is that possible?"

"She didn't have any marks on her that would explain her death," he said finally.

I blew out a sigh. "No marks?"

"Just two little marks by her throat," the younger officer volunteered from his spot where he was sitting on the couch rubbing Brittany's back as she sobbed uncontrollably.

"By her throat?" I shot a glance at Paris. She was staring off into space.

"Yeah, does that mean something to you?" Officer Obnoxious was trying to make eye contact with me. I didn't back down. I didn't want him to see weakness.

"No, it just sounds weird," I lied.

"That's what we thought, too."

"That obviously wasn't the cause of death," I said. "So, what was?"

The officer narrowed his eyes as he regarded me. "That's a weird question to ask."

"I told you, I watch a lot of television. Law and Order. CSI. Stuff like that." I left off the part about how much Dark Shadows I used to watch.

"All the blood from her body was drained."

"What?" Officer Obnoxious' answer took me by surprise – even though that's what I expected.

"All the blood in her body had been drained," he said again.

"Like a vampire?" Oh, great. Now Brittany was participating in the conversation.

"Vampires aren't real," the older cop scoffed.

Paris seemed to have snapped out of her funk. She shot a glance toward me and then turned her attention to Brittany.

"So what now?"

The older cop turned his attention back to me. "Now we contact her parents so they can hold a funeral and we wait for the full toxicology results."

"How long will that take?"

"It could take weeks," he admitted.

Great.

"Do you have your roommate's contact information for her parents?"

"No."

"Well, neither does the registrar."

"How can that be? We had to fill all that stuff out in the buckets full of paperwork when we applied."

"It must have been some clerical error, because there's no contact information in Ms. Thompson's file."

I pointed toward Tara's bunk and her part of the room. "Her stuff is over there."

The older officer made his way into the room and started going through her stuff. Obviously he didn't find what he was looking for. "There's nothing here."

"She probably kept her information in her phone like everyone else does. Just look in her phone."

"She wasn't found with a phone."

"She had one with her when we left last night."

"Are you sure?"

"Yes, I'm sure. We all had our phones."

"What kind of phone was it?"

"I think it was an Android," I said. "I can't be sure, though."

"It was an Android," Brittany piped up.

The police officer nodded. "We'll look again."

The younger officer had finally managed to extricate himself from a clingy Brittany. He moved toward the door with the other cop.

"If you can think of anything, give us a call," he said, slipping a card out of his pocket and handing it to me. Brittany looked disappointed he hadn't handed her the card. Even in death, she needed to be the center of attention.

After the two police officers left, I couldn't stop pacing. It was Sunday, but I knew exactly where I had to go.

I didn't shower. Instead I jumped in a pair of jeans, a T-shirt and a hoodie and tore out of the room. Paris didn't ask where I was going, but I could tell she knew exactly what was running through my mind.

I raced through campus – which was decidedly empty since it was Sunday – until I reached Professor Blake's office. The door was shut and I didn't bother knocking. I threw open the door dramatically and stepped into the room. He was sipping from a cup of coffee – and he didn't seem surprised to see me.

"I'm in."

31 THIRTY-ONE

The next day everyone went to classes as usual. I heard snatches of conversation here and there. Everyone was talking about the dead student and how she died. For her part, Brittany was making the most of the situation and crying on every cute boy's shoulder she could find. I was trying to ignore the situation – but it was literally everywhere around me.

"I heard she was stabbed twenty times."

"I heard she was gang raped on a pool table and then strangled."

"I heard she had her head bashed in by a brick."

The rumor mill at a school this size couldn't be trusted. That was the only thing I could rely on. No one really seemed to know how Tara had died.

After all three classes, I met Blake at the athletics center. He was waiting for me in the lobby. He hadn't asked a lot of questions the day before, but he also hadn't been surprised when I told him about Tara's death.

"I knew a student had died. I didn't realize it was your roommate, though."

He never offered his condolences. It both irked me and encouraged me at the same time. This wasn't about personal relationships. It was about action.

Once we made it to the other side of the security doors, I turned to Blake expectantly. "So what's up first?"

"I thought we'd ease you in today," he replied. "Just kind of a meet and greet with the other students and then a physical training session."

"Great." I tried to sound enthusiastic. It wasn't one of my better efforts.

Blake led me to a classroom at the far end of the basement corridor. Inside, there were about twenty different students. I followed Blake into the room. Professor Worth was lecturing from the front and she turned to greet Professor Blake with a flirtatious smile. Good grief.

I took the opportunity to look around the room. Unlike before, I did recognize one face in the crowd this time. Mark lifted up his head and met my gaze. His face broke into a wide grin when he saw me. What the hell?

Professor Worth introduced me to the class and then asked me to take a seat. I expected Blake to leave, but he sat in a chair in the corner instead.

"We were just talking about the murder the other night," Professor Worth said happily.

Professor Blake cleared his throat when he saw me glare at Professor Worth. She turned her apple-cheeked face to Blake expectantly. "The girl killed was Zoe's roommate," he supplied.

"Oh, I'm s-s-s-sorry," she stammered.

"It's fine," I dismissed her.

"No, you must be really upset."

"More like pissed off."

If Professor Worth was surprised by my vehemence, she didn't show it. "Well, what do you think happened?"

"I think a vampire killed her."

"Why do you think that?"

"She was drained of blood and the only marks on her body were on her throat. What else could it be?"

"How do you know that?" Professor Blake seemed curious.

"The cops that came to the room told us. Why?"

"We've been trying to get some definitive information on the attack, but we haven't been able to. I'm surprised they told you that."

I merely shrugged.

"Well, at least we know now."

"Why? What did you think it was?"

"We weren't sure," Professor Worth admitted.

"Then how did you know it was a supernatural?"

"What else would it be?" She asked simply.

"Humans kill humans, too."

"Not around here," she laughed.

"Oh, that's a bunch of crap."

Professor Worth looked taken aback. "Now listen here young lady ... ."

"No, you listen. I don't believe for a second that there is no human-on-human violence here. If that's the load of bull you're selling, then I'm not buying."

"Then why are you here?" Professor Blake asked.

"Because a vampire killed my roommate. I want to kill the vampire that did it."

"We want to kill all of them!" This came from a blonde boy in the back row. The rest of the class erupted in agreement. A couple of guys even got up from their seats and high-fived the loud mouth with all a wave of bravado.

"That's enough, Brian," Professor Worth warned.

"Yes, that's enough Brian," I mocked.

Brian glared at me. His cool blue eyes were suddenly regarding me as the enemy. Good.

Brian got to his feet and swaggered over to me. He reminded me of Cato in The Hunger Games for some reason. I bet he was just as much of a dick. "Listen, little lady, I've been doing this for a year now.

I've seen things that would make a little girl like you crawl under her bed and hide for a week."

Mark sucked in a breath as he turned to me. I'd only known him for two weeks, but he knew I wasn't going to take that lying down.

"Really? Because I've been attacked by a vampire that I had to kill and went to a wolf pack meeting."

"You're lying," Brian protested.

Professor Blake jumped to his feet and moved to my side. "What wolf pack meeting?"

Uh-oh.

"Um, that was just a figure of speech," I offered lamely.

Professor Blake's eyes narrowed. "What aren't you telling me?"

"What aren't you telling me?"

"Her boyfriend is a member of Alpha Chi," Mark offered.

I turned to him and glared openly.

"You didn't tell me that," Professor Blake admonished me. "You were dating a werewolf?"

Everyone in the room looked at me in a different light all of a sudden. Now I truly was the enemy.

"I didn't know he was a werewolf," I argued. "I broke up with him when I found out. How do you even know about the frat?"

The class dissolved into giggles.

"We've been monitoring them for quite some time," Professor Blake said. "I wish I had known about your boyfriend. We could have used your proximity to infiltrate them."

"And why would I want to do that?"

"We want to know what they're up to."

"They're drugging girls and playing video games."

Professor Blake looked surprised. "What do you mean drugging girls?"

"I mean they've drugged at least two girls I know of."

"Why didn't you tell me?"

"You didn't ask."

Professor Blake looked nonplussed. "That's no excuse."

"Hey! I hadn't decided if I could trust you yet." Honestly, I still hadn't decided. The only reason I'd owned up to the fact that Alpha Chi was full of werewolves was because they already seemed to know. There was no sense in lying about the situation.

Professor Blake blew out a sigh. "I understand that but ... ."

"But what?"

"But this situation is bigger than you."

After the information exchange, Professor Worth dismissed the class and Professor Blake led everyone to the gym. After a brief work-out, he paired us off in twos to spar. Thankfully, I got Mark.

"So you've been keeping secrets," I said to him.

"You, too," he smiled.

"How long have you been a part of this?"

"Just a week," he said. "They recruited me, too."

"Why?"

Mark looked hurt. "I didn't mean that the way it sounded," I offered.

"They want my computer skills," Mark answered.

"Why?"

"I don't know. They haven't told me yet."

"Doesn't that make you nervous?"

Mark shrugged. "No."

"Do you believe in all this?" I motioned around the room.

"Do I believe in fighting monsters? Yeah. Don't you?"

"Fighting monsters? Yes. What if they're not all monsters, though?"

"Like Will?"

I was thinking more of Aric and Rafael, but I didn't want to tip my hand. "Yeah, like Will."

"If he's not a monster, why did you break up with him?"

"I didn't break up with him because he's a wolf. I broke up with him because he's a sheep."

"What do you mean?"

"I mean that he completely stopped being himself and started being just like them. That's not the guy I knew."

I took advantage of Mark's thoughtful expression to flip him over my back and toss him on the mats below me. I pinned him quickly. "There are all types of monsters Mark. They're not all supernatural."

I got up and started to move out of the room. I caught Professor Blake watching me. I paused, just for a second, and then walked out into the hallway. I desperately needed some air.

Unfortunately, Blake had followed me. "You're leaving?"

"Just getting some air."

"Are you hiding anything else from us?"

"No."

"Are you sure?" Professor Blake's gaze was probing.

"What do you want from me?"

"Your allegiance. You're too important to not be a part of this."

"What does that mean?"

"It means that you have a natural ability. That's something the rest of these people don't have. They have oodles of enthusiasm, but no ability. You have no enthusiasm, but tons of ability."

I didn't know how to respond, so instead I studied my cuticles. I could definitely use a manicure.

"We can't afford for you to join the other side, Zoe."

I raised my eyes and met Professor Blake's steady gaze. "I'm not joining any side. I'm here to make sure that the monster that killed Tara doesn't kill anyone else."

"And then what?"

"What do you mean?"

"After you get one monster, are you willing to let all the other monsters live?"

"Who decides who the monsters are? You?"

"You seem to think it's you."

"I don't know who is and who isn't a monster," I admitted. "I just don't think that being a werewolf or a vampire necessarily makes you a monster."

"What do you mean by that?"

"Maybe they're like humans. Maybe there are good vampires and good werewolves."

"That's a simplistic thought."

"Or maybe it's just logic."

I didn't wait for Professor Blake's response. Instead I trotted down the dark hallway. I didn't stop until I reached the light outside.

32 THIRTY-TWO

After returning to the dorms, I told Paris about my afternoon.

"I'm not sure joining up with them is a good idea," she admitted.

"I'm not sure either."

"Then why did you do it?"

"Knee-jerk reaction to Tara's death?"

"You can still get out of it."

"Can I?"

Paris and I decided that we needed a mundane evening, so we hauled our laundry to the basement. Thankfully, it was empty except for Mark. I hadn't told Paris that Mark was part of the monster-fighting academy yet. I didn't figure it was my secret to tell.

Mark didn't seem to be embracing all the secret society nonsense, though.

"Did you tell her about kicking my ass this afternoon?"

Paris' eyebrows nearly shot off her forehead. "You're a part of the academy?"

"You didn't tell her?" Mark seemed surprised.

"I didn't feel it was my place," I grumbled.

Mark's enthusiasm couldn't be dampened. He launched into a long – and extremely tedious – story about how Professor Worth had seen his work in the computer lab and recruited him.

"Didn't you think it was weird?"

Mark shrugged. "I don't know. I just thought it sounded cool. Like a really awesome comic book or something."

Men.

"Did Zoe tell you she's the star of the class?" Mark asked innocently.

Paris slid a look my way. "No."

"Well, she is. Everyone is in awe of her, even the people that have been part of the group for years. No one knows what to make of her, especially since Professor Blake is trying so hard to recruit her."

"Why do you think they want Zoe so bad?"

Mark took a bite of the candy bar he had pulled from his pocket and chewed thoughtfully.

"I don't know. She seems like a natural or something, I guess."

God was I sick of hearing that.

"What types of things do they teach you?" Paris was curious. I didn't blame her.

"Just about the history of stuff. Like how vampires came to be."

"How did they come to be?"

"Some guy thought he was a vampire so he drank so much blood he became one. He launched the race."

"That doesn't make any sense," I argued.

"That's what they say," Mark shrugged.

"Do you believe that?"

"I don't know. I just know that monsters are real – and they're here – and we have to stop them."

Paris and I exchanged dubious looks.

"What if they're not all monsters?" I asked.

"What do you mean?"

"Just because they're werewolves and vampires, that doesn't mean they're all monsters."

"What else could they be?"

"Maybe they're just different kinds of people trying to survive?"

"Yeah, but they survive by killing people."

"Not werewolves."

Mark seemed to consider my statement for a second. Then he shrugged again.

"And if vampires were really killing people to survive, wouldn't there be a lot more deaths?"

"That's a good question," Paris offered.

"I never really thought about it like that," Mark admitted.

"No, I don't think Blake wants you to," I muttered.

"If you don't like him, why are you joining the cause?"

"I'm not joining the cause. I'm trying to find out who killed Tara."

"Are you quitting after that?"

"I don't know."

I turned back to the washing machine and transferred my wet clothes to the dryer. When I was done, I turned back to Paris and Mark. They had their heads bent together and were smiling at one another. I had a feeling Paris' breakup with Mike would be happening sooner rather than later.

"So have Tara's parents come by and picked up her stuff?" Mark asked.

I was surprised by the question. The more I thought about it, though, I had no idea why.

"No. That's weird though, isn't it?"

Paris seemed to mull the thought over, too. "You know, not only have we not heard anything from Tara's parents, but we haven't heard anything from the cops either."

"Has Brittany?"

"Not that I know of."

"Even if they were too upset to come get her stuff, you'd think they'd send someone. Or have someone call us."

"Do we even know that she has parents?"

"Everyone has parents," Paris said.

"I mean, maybe they're dead or something. Did she ever talk about her parents?"

Paris thought back for a second. "I don't remember her mentioning them."

"What about when she moved in?"

"She was the last to arrive and she was alone."

"Didn't she have a boyfriend?"

"Yeah. She mentioned having one that first night, but she never really brought him up again."

"Did you ever see her call him?"

"No."

"Me neither."

After finishing our laundry, we all went up to the dorm room. I pulled out my iPad and sat down on the couch.

"What are you doing?"

"Googling Tara."

Unfortunately, Tara Thompson wasn't exactly a unique name. The search came back with thousands of results.

"We have to narrow this down. What did she say her hometown was?"

"Zilwaukee."

"Zilwaukee? That doesn't make sense. That's only a half an hour away. Why wouldn't she save the money and commute?"

"Maybe she wanted to live in the dorms?"

"Maybe."

I added Zilwaukee to the search parameters and came up with nothing. "Are we sure it was Zilwaukee?"

"Yeah, you made that joke about the Zilwaukee Bridge."

"What joke?"

"I don't remember now."

"It mustn't have been very funny.

"It wasn't."

I bit my lip to keep from smiling. I didn't think that it was appropriate to laugh when you were searching for information about your dead roommate.

"See if you can find any Thompsons in Zilwaukee," Paris suggested. "It's a small town. There can't be that many."

"There's one."

"Let's call them."

I pulled out my phone and dialed the number I found. The voice at the other end sounded old. Very old.

"I'm sorry to bother you," I started. "Um, well, here's the thing, our roommate died the other day and she said she was from Zilwaukee and you're the only Thompsons I could find in Zilwaukee."

"I'm a little old to have a daughter in college, dear," the old lady on the other end of the phone said. I didn't doubt it.

"Maybe a granddaughter? Her name was Tara."

"I don't know any Tara," the woman answered.

"Are there any other Thompsons in Zilwaukee?"

"Not that I know of."

I thanked the woman for her time and disconnected. "Why would Tara lie about where she lived?"

"Maybe she didn't lie. Maybe she lived with her stepfather or something and her mom has a different last name or something."

"That's possible."

Still, something about the situation bothered me. I just couldn't put my finger on it.

"Maybe they're just unlisted?"

"Maybe."

"Maybe they only have a cellphone and that wouldn't necessarily show up in public records. A lot of people are eliminating landlines."

This was true. Still.

I blew out a breath. "Maybe she's not from Zilwaukee?"

Paris bit her lip. "But why would she lie?"

Why indeed?

33 THIRTY-THREE

The next day I was still troubled by the fact that we could find no record of Tara in Zilwaukee. I thought about talking to Professor Blake about it – but the truth was, I didn't trust him. Instead, I decided to give Aric a call. Okay, maybe I didn't fully trust him either. He was just so much better looking.

After laying out what we had found, Aric told me to wait at the dorms. I told him I would be waiting for him in the parking lot.

"I'll pick you up at your room."

"It's not a big deal, I'll just meet you downstairs."

"I said that I will pick you up in your room."

This went on for five minutes before I finally acquiesced. I didn't know what his deal was – but I didn't think fighting about where he would pick me up was the best use of our time.

While I was waiting in the living room, Paris eyed me questioningly and Brittany burrowed under a comforter and continued to fake freak out. I didn't know who she was trying to impress -- especially since the door to the hall was shut – but she was giving the performance of a lifetime.

"What are you all dressed up for?"

I looked down at my outfit confused. Lucky jeans – that admittedly hugged my butt in just the right way – a Star Wars shirt and my purple slip-on converse. Typical outfit – that I always made look good. Did that sound stuck up?

"The only reason to wear Lucky jeans is if you plan on unzipping them."

This was true.

"And your Mark Ecko glittery *Star Wars* shirt? You're pulling out the big guns."

"What do you mean by that?"

"I mean your boobs look huge in that shirt."

Ah, that's what she means.

"I just happened to grab the first thing I saw," I lied.

"I guess you just lucked out," Paris was smirking at me as I checked out my reflection one more time in the full-length mirror.

Luckily for us the conversation couldn't digress any further. There was a sharp rap on the door. I reached over and opened it.

For a second, it was like all the air was sucked out of the room. Aric stepped in with little ceremony – and yet I couldn't help but hear the theme to Star Wars suddenly play in my head. How he could make simple jeans, a tank top and a blue flannel look so appealing was beyond me.

Paris must have realized that I wasn't speaking – mostly because I was so busy internally drooling – so she decided to fill the conversational gap. "You look nice, Aric."

I noticed Brittany had perked up on the couch and was running her fingers through her snarled hair. She should have tried running some shampoo through it, too.

Aric looked confused. "I always look like this."

Paris smiled. "I bet you do."

I grabbed Aric's arm and pulled him out the door, tossing Paris a cursory wave behind my back as we went.

"Where are you going?" Brittany asked.

I paused and turned back. "We're going to Zilwaukee to see if we can find anyone that knew Tara."

"That sounds like fun. If you wait, I'll get showered and go with you?"

Paris shot Brittany a look. "I think they're fine going by themselves."

Brittany either didn't seem to notice Paris' not-so-subtle hint or didn't care. "We can cover more ground with three people."

Aric took a long look at Brittany as she got to her feet. He took in her flannel pajamas, snarled hair and runny nose and immediately started shaking his head.

"I have a truck," he offered. "There's only room for two of us."

Brittany look disappointed. As we shut the door, I heard Paris smack the back of Brittany's head. "You idiot."

"What?" Brittany whined.

"You don't horn in on someone else's date."

"I didn't think it was a date."

"Look at him. Of course it's a date."

I shut the door and turned to see Aric's reaction. He was eyeing me with a wolfish grin. "This is a date?"

"I didn't say that. Paris said that. I know you don't think it's a date."

Aric followed me down the hall quietly. "If this isn't a date, it's too bad you had to break out the tight jeans and your very special Star Wars shirt."

I swung around to see the merriment in his eyes. "I'll have you know, all of my Star Wars shirts are very special."

When we got down to the parking lot, Aric led me to his Ford pickup truck. It wasn't exactly new – but it did have a cool retro feel to it. It was slate gray, and the interior was a well-worn black leather. It felt comfortable. As I slid into the passenger seat, I couldn't help but be relieved that the cab was clearly too small for the two of us to have sex in, because for some reason all I could think about was getting out of my tight jeans and running my fingers through his thick black hair.

I turned to Aric and – I swear – it seemed like he was reading my mind. His gaze looked hot for a second – and then it was replaced by a sly smirk. I decided to ignore him.

"What?"

"Nothing."

"I know what you were thinking."

"What was I thinking?"

"That you wanted check out my X-Wing."

Aric looked confused for a second – and then my double entendre must have become clear. "That's the first time anyone has ever propositioned me with a *Star Wars* analogy."

"That wasn't a proposition."

"What was it?"

"When it's a proposition – you'll know it's a proposition."

"I can't wait."

The ride to Zilwaukee was boring. Thankfully, it wasn't too long. I had never been to Zilwaukee, so I wasn't sure what to expect. I'm glad I wasn't expecting too much. I definitely would have been disappointed.

Aric and I parked at a local diner. There weren't a lot of options – and this was the first place we found that wasn't akin to an armpit made out of wood and abandoned vehicles.

"This place is bleak," Aric said.

"Compared to what?"

"Compared to everything."

I couldn't agree more.

We made our way into the diner and found a table. To no one's surprise – especially mine – it was sticky.

"So what's the plan?" I was trying to keep my elbows from the table while I searched my purse for a wet nap. Maybe we should have brought Brittany, after all. She always had wet naps.

"We have lunch, feel out the room and then ask about Tara."

"We're eating here?"

"Don't be such a snob," Aric admonished me.

"Just because I'm worried about eating road kill does not make me a snob."

Aric gave me a warning look as the waitress came to the table. I couldn't help but smile when I took in her orange polyester uniform, acrylic nails and ratted hair. The 1980s had officially came to this town – and never left.

I watched Aric smile winningly at the waitress. "What are your specials?"

I noticed that the waitress had straightened her previously bent posture and was now pushing her ample boobs into Aric's face. He didn't look impressed.

"Well, honey, we have chicken pot pie on special today."

Yuck.

"I'll have a cheeseburger with everything and fries," Aric smiled.

"You got it, sweetheart," the waitress started to move away.

"What about me?"

The waitress swung around. "Oh, sorry, honey, I forgot all about you. What do you want?"

I couldn't help but notice that the waitress – who had a nametag that read Fern – was looking at Aric and smiling flirtatiously.

"I'll have a chicken sandwich with lettuce and tomato and an order of fries," I grumbled.

After Fern left I turned to Aric expectantly. "What was that?"

"What was what?"

"You and the waitress."

"I was placing an order."

"Oh please."

"You're cute when you're jealous."

"I'm not jealous of someone named Fern that is stuck in the 80s."

Aric just smiled knowingly.

When our lunch came, I was surprised at how good it looked. "This looks great," I said to Fern.

"This is the best restaurant in town."

"How many restaurants are there?"

"This is the only one."

"So it's the best and worst restaurant in town at the same time," I laughed at my own joke.

"What?"

"Nothing."

After we ate, Aric called Fern over. "Actually, Fern, we're here looking for someone." His voice was friendly – but the minute he opened his mouth Fern's demeanor changed.

"Are you a cop?"

"No."

"Then why are you looking for someone?"

Aric paused for a second. He clearly didn't know how to proceed.

"We're students at Covenant," I supplied. "My roommate was killed the other night. She said she was from Zilwaukee. We just want to pay our condolences to her family."

It wasn't exactly a lie. It wasn't exactly the truth either.

Fern looked genuinely surprised. She turned her full attention to me for the first time since we came into the diner. "That is awful."

I pulled my phone out and showed Fern a picture of Tara. "Her name is Tara Thompson."

Fern took the phone from me and stared at the photo a second. She looked confused. I figured that was a perpetual state for her.

"Do you know her?"

"Yeah, I know her."

"You do?" Despite myself I was surprised. I figured this was going to be a dead end. "Do you know where we can find Tara's parents?"

"Why do you keep calling her Tara?"

"What do you mean?"

"That's not her name."

"What's her name?" Aric asked.

"That's Lola," Fern said.

"Lola? Lola Thompson?"

"No, Lola Winters."

I was actually speechless.

"How do you know Lola?" Aric seemed to be looking for a specific answer.

"We went to school together."

I looked Fern up and down again. She looked forty.

"That can't be right," I said carefully. "Tara ... I mean Lola ... was twenty-two."

"No, Lola was thirty-eight."

I shook my camera in front of Fern again. "This girl was not thirty-eight. Are you sure it's Lola?"

"Yeah, I'm sure although," Fern bit her bottom lip in obvious confusion.

"Although what?"

"I haven't seen Lola since we graduated from high school and she looks exactly the same. How can that be?"

"Maybe Lola has a daughter?"

"Maybe." Fern didn't seem convinced. "They look exactly alike, though."

"Lots of daughters look like their moms," I supplied.

"Not like twins, though," Fern said.

I turned to look at Aric. For his part, he seemed lost in thought.

"When was the last time you saw Lola?"

"High school graduation," Fern said.

"Were you friends?"

"It's a small town. Everyone knew each other. No one was really friends with Lola, though."

"Why?"

"She was just ... different."

"Different how?"

"You know, she was just weird. No one really liked her."

"What? Did she sit in the back of the room and eat her hair? Was she a bully? How was she different?"

"I don't know," Fern seemed put off by my aggressive questions. "She was just different. She dressed all in black. People say she was a witch."

"A witch? Like she was obnoxious to be around?"

"No, like she went out into the woods and sacrificed animals."

"She sacrificed animals?"

"I mean, I never saw her do it. That was just the rumor."

I looked to Aric for help. He was still lost in his own thoughts.

"Is Lola's family still around?"

Fern thought for a second and then shook her head. "No. Her mom left when she did and that was her only family."

"What about her father?"

"I never met her father. I'm not even sure she ever met him. She sure never talked about him."

Fern didn't have any more information. Aric paid our bill and we silently went back out to his truck. When we climbed into the cab, I turned to him. "What does this mean?"

"I don't know."

"Are witches real?"

Aric shrugged. It was like he was tuning me out.

"Why are you being so quiet all of a sudden?"

"Just thinking," Aric replied absently.

The rest of the ride back to the school didn't go much better. When we got to the dorms, he didn't even bother saying goodbye to me.

As I exited the truck I turned to him.

"I don't know what your deal is, but I don't appreciate being frozen out here."

"I'm not freezing you out. I'm thinking."

I met Aric's eyes for a minute. As I did, I realized he was lying. I didn't know what about – or even how I knew he was lying -- I just knew.

"Fine!"

I slammed the door shut and stormed into the building.

I didn't turn around to see if Aric watched me enter the building. I was beyond caring at this point.

34 THIRTY-FOUR

T he next few weeks were uneventful.

The school packed up Tara's belongings and took them away. I never found out where.

I'd stayed away from Aric and Rafael. I was done with men. What? I was.

I was also done with Professor Blake's little monster school, too. At least for now. He had questioned me about my reticence. I admitted that I wasn't ready to join the cause. In truth, I didn't know if I believed in his cause. There are monsters and there are monsters. As irritated as I was with Rafael – and especially Aric – I didn't believe they were monsters. The jury was still out on Professor Blake.

Life slowly reverted to normal. I got in a groove with my classes. Paris finally broke up with Mike and she and Mark were flirting incessantly. Brittany had even gotten her swagger back and was back to stalking Rick No. 1 in the dorm hallway – which wasn't going over well with Matilda. She was spending more time with the girls down the hall – which I encouraged.

Homecoming weekend was upon us – and while I didn't care about football, I was up for a fun party.

"I'm going to the Alpha Chi party," Brittany announced.

I couldn't believe it. "Don't you remember what happened last time?"

"Yes, but we don't know it was them."

"We don't know it wasn't them either. Why would you take that chance?"

"Even if one of them did it, that doesn't mean all of them are behind it," Brittany huffed.

I figured that was code for "these are the hottest guys on campus."

"You're on your own tonight," I cautioned her. "I'm not going to rescue you."

"I don't need you to rescue me."

Right.

Brittany decided to get ready with the girls down the hall. I don't think she liked the dark looks I kept shooting at her. Good.

After she left, Paris seemed to be tip-toeing around me. She clearly had something to say to me and wasn't sure how to approach it.

"What?" I finally exploded.

"You know we can't let her go to that party alone."

"I don't know that."

"Zoe, come on. It's too dangerous. She's an easy mark."

"She makes herself an easy mark."

"I know she does. Are you going to be able to forgive yourself if something happens to her?"

"I'll throw a party."

Paris gave me a disappointed look. "I don't believe that."

I blew out a sigh. Neither did I.

I grudgingly agreed to go to the party with Paris. "If she does one stupid thing I'm going to drag her out of there by her bottle blonde hair."

"Look at it this way," Paris soothed. "We can use the party as an excuse to snoop around and see what they're doing."

"Why would I want to do that?"

Paris looked at me with mild disbelief.

"What?"

"You're a busybody."

"I am not a busybody."

"Yes you are."

I was quiet for a minute. "If we sneak around we have to be careful about it. If they catch us, things could go south quick."

Paris smirked.

"I am not a busybody," I muttered.

We watched television in silence for a while. Paris finally spoke. "What are you going to wear?"

"Jeans and a T-shirt."

"Your good jeans and your good T-shirt?"

"I don't know, why?"

"Well, Aric will probably be there ... ."

"So," I bristled. I hadn't spoken to Aric since he had turned into a block of ice and dropped me off in front of the dorms. Screw Aric.

"I'm just saying, he'll probably be there."

"Well, good for him," I grumbled.

Paris gave me a knowing look. I wasn't that fond of her right now, either.

The Homecoming game was at 6 p.m. Paris and I declined to go. I was even happier about that choice when I saw Brittany and her new friends walk down the hallway with their faces painted and clad in college sweatshirts. It looked like the school had thrown up their own colors and it had landed on certain people. Blech.

Paris and I got ready for the party. Brittany and her new friends were going right from the game to the party. I couldn't wait to see what that face paint looked like after a few beers.

When we got to the party, I was surprised to see that the entire frat house had been decorated for Halloween – which was a full week away.

"Looks like they're in the holiday spirit," Paris mused.

Personally, I found the purple lights, gruesome pumpkins and spider webs creepy. Maybe it was just creepy because the fraternity brothers were spending their days drugging women? That's all I could think about for a second, though, that the frat brothers were trying to catch these women in their web.

There was a large bonfire in the backyard, and that's where Paris and I headed. We had brought our own beer. We weren't taking any chances.

When we got to the backyard, we each popped open a bottle and surveyed the situation. It looked like a giant orgy to me. Couples were either freaking on the makeshift dance floor or pawing each other in the darkened corners.

My gaze landed on Brittany – and I felt like the wind had been knocked out of me. She had changed her clothes between the game and the party. She was wearing a low-cut top and she was flirting like a madwoman. Unfortunately she was flirting with Will.

Paris followed my gaze and swallowed hard.

"I'm going to kill her," I seethed.

"Don't make a scene."

"Why not? She deserves it."

"Yes, she does. We don't want to draw attention to ourselves."

I was genuinely torn. Paris had a point. It could be dangerous to draw attention to ourselves. Brittany was a flaming slut, though. My rage won out.

I stomped up to Brittany and gave her a pointed look. She looked surprised to see me. "What are you doing here?"

"Partying. What are you doing?"

"Just hanging out." Brittany looked uncomfortable. She was going to be a lot more uncomfortable when I put my boot up her ass.

For his part, Will had the grace to look embarrassed. "You shouldn't be here," he said in a low voice.

I couldn't help but notice the victorious look that shot across Brittany's face.

"Don't worry, I won't be here long," I said.

"If they see you ... ." Will seemed conflicted.

"If who sees her?" Brittany looked confused.

"I'm not here for them," I answered shortly. "I just wanted to make sure no one drugged Brittany's drink and took advantage of her."

Brittany looked surprised – and touched.

"Don't get too excited," I turned to her. "I'm over any protective feelings."

"What is that supposed to mean?" She looked offended.

"You don't go after your roommate's ex-boyfriend," I said bitterly.

"I wasn't going after him," Brittany lied. "We were just talking. I can't help it if he's interested me."

"I'm not interested in her," Will said hastily.

Brittany looked offended. Good.

"How can you not be interested in me?" Brittany was bordering on shrill. "You can't possibly still be interested in her!"

What was that supposed to mean?

"She's a total bitch and she was a total bitch to you," Brittany continued.

"That's not exactly what happened," Will said, looking at his feet.

Well, at least he wasn't throwing me under the bus.

"We were both at fault," he said.

"How was I at fault?"

"You know how you were at fault," Will looked around nervously. "Keep your voice down."

"You know what? You're right." Will looked surprised. "I'm done. I'm so done here. I'm going to find Paris and we're going to leave. We won't be back."

I saw Brittany start bitching at Will as I left. "Do you think she's prettier than me?"

Will looked like he would rather be just about anywhere than where he was right now.

Paris was still standing where I left her. Unfortunately, Aric was standing beside her. I couldn't hear what they were saying. Paris saw me approaching, though. "How did that go?"

"Just how you would expect."

Aric turned to greet me. The smile that had been plastered on his face disappeared when he saw the anger radiating from me. "What's wrong?"

"Oh, now you care?"

"What is that supposed to mean?"

"I haven't heard from you in weeks!"

"You could have called me, too. Or does your phone only receive calls?"

"Why would I do that when you were the one lying and acting like an asshole?"

"I wasn't acting like an asshole."

"But you were lying, weren't you?"

Aric averted his gaze from me. "I don't know what you're talking about."

"Huh, another lie."

I grabbed Paris' arm and started to drag her away. "We're leaving."

"What about Brittany?"

"She's on her own."

Paris looked like she was going to argue and then changed her mind and followed me. Aric just watched us go.

When we got to the front of the buildings, I swerved to the building on the left – the empty one.

"Where are we going?"

"Shh."

I looked around to see if anyone was watching us. Thankfully, everyone was still in the backyard. "We're looking around."

"Now?"

"Yes."

"They know we're here, though," she said.

"I'm done caring."

I walked up the steps and opened the front door and stepped inside. Paris looked like she was going to balk at first, but then resignation washed over her pale features. She followed me inside. Neither one of us could have been prepared for what we were about to see – or rather the person we were about to see.

"Omigod, Tara," Paris exclaimed.

Tara looked as surprised to see us as we were to see her.

"What are you doing here? We have to hide."

35 THIRTY-FIVE

Tara dragged Paris and me into the room roughly, glancing nervously outside before shutting the door behind us.

"What are you doing here?" She turned on us abruptly.

"Looking to see what they're up to," I admitted. I saw no sense in lying. There was no lie I could make up that would be plausible.

"You shouldn't have come here," she said, looking between us. "Especially you," she said nodding at me.

"Because I know what they are?"

"Because you know what we all are."

Paris looked surprised. "You're a wolf, too?"

"I see you told her."

"She's trustworthy," I said.

"I know she is. Where's Brittany?"

"She's outside – being not so trustworthy," I responded.

If she was curious, Tara kept her questions to herself. "You need to get out of here."

"No way! I want some answers."

"I don't have time to give you any," Tara argued.

"Do you really think we're going to just let our dead roommate walk away? Well, walk away again?"

Tara sighed. "I'm sorry you had to go through that, but there was no way around it."

"Why don't you start at the beginning," Paris prodded.

Tara looked like she wanted to argue. One look at our determined faces, though, and she decided against it.

"I had no choice," she said. "I had to fake my death."

"Why?"

"I was in danger."

"From who?"

"The vampires."

"What vampires?" I feigned ignorance.

"Don't," Tara admonished me. "We don't have time for this. I know you know. Everyone knows you know."

"How does everyone know that?"

"We are just as aware of what Blake and his cronies are up to as he is of what is going on throughout this campus."

I didn't tell her that Blake really had no idea what was going on – especially at the Alpha Chi house. Or, at least he had no idea until I told him. I doubted that little admission would win any points with her.

"If everyone knows about each other, then why don't they just confront each other?"

Tara shrugged. "That would be too easy, I guess."

"Why did you fake your death?" Paris asked.

"I told you, I had to protect myself. It wasn't planned. When I saw Rafael in the bar, though, I knew I was in trouble."

"Rafael?"

"You know him?" Tara narrowed her eyes.

"Yeah," I admitted. "He keeps showing up."

"Where did you first meet him?"

"Mike's party – that first night we went there."

Tara looked surprised. "I was at that party and I didn't see him."

"He was on the balcony."

"Did you know he was a vampire?"

"Not then," I admitted.

"When did you find out?"

"After Blake took me to his monster academy."

"And that was after the incident at the frat house?"

"Well, actually ... ."

"Well, actually what?"

"I've been there a couple times," I said. "The first time was before the incident at the frat house."

"What did he want from you?"

"To join the cause," I said simply.

"That makes sense," Tara said. "They've always wanted you because of where you come from."

"Everyone keeps saying that, and yet I had no idea any of that was supposedly going on," I said. "I didn't know about wolves."

"I find that hard to believe."

"Well, it's true."

Tara looked at me dubiously.

"It's true. I had no idea. Even when Blake told me about it I still had trouble believing it."

Tara shook her head. "I don't know why you would be kept in the dark – and we don't have time to figure that out."

"What do you mean?"

"Zoe, I can't protect you from the pack," she said. "I'm not in charge. I have no pull. They're already irritated with me about faking my death."

"How did you do that, by the way?" Paris asked.

"It wasn't easy."

"You want to expand on that?"

"Not right now. It's too long of a story."

"What are you going to do now?"

"Move," she said simply. "Again."

"Where are you going to move?"

"Some place where I can be safe."

"Where is that?"

"I don't know. I just want to go to school and be a normal person. I don't want to be in all this pack crap. I don't want to be threatened by vampires. I just want to be a person."

"Why are the vampires after you?"

"I don't even know if they know anymore," Tara admitted. "For as long as I've been alive I've just been told to hide from vampires because they want to wipe us all out."

"But why?"

"I honestly don't know," she said. "It's a grudge match, if you ask me. Both their kind and our kind want to be the reigning kings of the hill. It's ridiculous."

"Why don't you, I don't know, have designated wolf areas and designated vampire areas? I mean, that wouldn't solve the Blake problem, but that would solve the other problem."

"That's the way I was for years," Tara explained. "The thing is, without someone to fight, wolves get bored."

"And vampires?"

"I don't know them well enough to speak for them."

We all froze when we heard a door open at the back of the house. Tara looked terrified. She pushed us toward the front door. "Go. I'll find you when I can to say goodbye."

The look on her face was enough to convince me, so Paris and I disappeared through the front door. We looked around furtively and crossed the street. No one had seen us. When we made it to the end of the block, I pulled Paris into the bushes and forced her to crouch down alongside me.

"What are we doing?"

"Waiting."

"Why?"

"I want to see what happens."

We waited and waited and waited – for what seemed like hours.

In reality, it was probably only fifteen minutes. That's when the door Paris and I had escaped through opened again.

This time it was Tara that stepped out. She looked around. Not seeing anyone, she anxiously started down the sidewalk. Paris looked like she was going to stand and go after Tara, but I grabbed her and pulled her back down. I put my finger to my lips to warn her to be silent. She looked perplexed, but did as I told her to.

When Tara reached the corner, she turned it quickly, heading away from us. I waited about two minutes and then stood up and started to cross the street after her.

"Where are we going?" Paris whispered.

"We're following her."

"Why?"

"Because her story doesn't make any sense."

"I know it doesn't. She didn't have time to explain."

"No, she didn't want to explain. She didn't want us to find her."

"What makes you think that?"

"Just call it intuition."

Paris looked doubtful but followed me.

"Where do you think she's going?"

"Someplace we can get answers."

"Where's that?"

"I honestly don't know."

36 THIRTY-SIX

Paris and I trailed a full two blocks behind Tara. We knew we ran the risk of losing her in the dark – but neither of us was stealthy enough to pull any closer. Luckily, we didn't have that far to travel.

Tara wasn't embarking on some long trek. In fact, she merely made a wide loop around the property. I realized, when she skirted into a darkened building, that the house she had entered backed up to the back of the Alpha Chi property.

Paris and I both huddled underneath a tree across the road from the house. We weren't sure how to proceed.

"What do you think?" Paris asked.

"I think that this all feels like a weird set-up," I admitted.

"What makes you say that? The fact that we just ran into our dead roommate and that she suspiciously walked out of a frat house that is filled with wolves, but she only went around the block and entered a dark house that is probably filled with certain doom?"

"Sarcasm isn't going to help us at this point," I chastised.

"Who was being sarcastic?"

I bit my lower lip as I looked at the house. I wasn't sure what to do. I knew entering the house was a stupid idea – but I couldn't exactly walk away either.

"Why don't we sneak around and see if we can see in through a window?" Paris offered.

"That's a good idea."

"No it's not – but I know you won't leave and I don't want to try and sneak into the house."

We quietly made our way toward the house, slipping inside the hedge on the left side of the structure before we got to the front porch. I was hopeful no one in the house was staring out the window. If they were, everything we were about to do was a waste of time.

The first window was dark – and dirty. I wrapped the lip of my hoodie over my wrist and tried to clear a small area so we could see into the house. As far as I could tell, there was nothing in the room. It was so dark, though, I couldn't be certain.

We shuffled down to the next window – but we didn't have any luck there either.

"Let's go to the back of the house," Paris whispered.

I nodded and we moved further down the side of the house. In my attempt to be quiet, I should have paid more attention, because my shoe snagged on the root of the hedge as I tried to move into the backyard and I sprawled out into the open. Probably not my best move, especially since there were about thirty wolves watching me as I brushed the knees of my jeans off and looked up. Paris rushed out to help me and froze when she saw all the eyes focused on us.

Tara was standing in the middle of the wolves. She didn't look surprised to see us. In fact, she looked satisfied.

"I knew you couldn't just go home," she said smugly.

"We wanted to make sure you were alright," Paris whispered.

"I didn't," I offered. "I just wanted to see what you were up to."

Tara smirked. "I bet you wish you had just let it go?"

"Not particularly," I lied.

"Don't worry," she soothed. "You will."

Tara motioned to the wolves and they surrounded Paris and me. There really was no sense of running off. We'd never make it.

I put up a minimal struggle when a couple of sets of rough hands grabbed my arms. "Let go of me, dog breath," I seethed.

Tara pointed to a picnic table on the far side of the property. "Go sit there and shut up," she ordered.

"I will go over there and sit – but only because my knee hurts," I sniffed.

Paris kicked my shin. "Stop antagonizing them."

"Why? They're going to kill us anyway."

"She's not wrong," Tara said, her eyes hardening.

"Why not just do it now?" Paris asked Tara. I think she was still appealing to Tara's sense of humanity. I was fairly certain that -- if Tara ever had any humanity – it was long gone.

"It's not your turn yet," Tara supplied.

"Whose turn is it?" Paris asked, her voice sounded like a squeak more than anything else. Tara ignored her.

"Your name is Lola, isn't it?" I don't know why I said it. If there was even a chance of us getting out of here, I had just blown it. I never did know when to keep my mouth shut.

Tara froze in surprise. "Who told you that?"

"I went to Zilwaukee." Might as well let it all out.

"Why would you do that?" I could tell Tara was angry. She was just barely controlling her rage.

"We couldn't figure out why no one came to pick up your stuff," I said honestly. "We wanted to send our condolences to your parents. Then we realized that you never mentioned your parents."

"So you went to Zilwaukee?"

"Not right away. We Googled you first."

"You Googled me?"

"And when we came up with nothing we thought that was weird – so I went to Zilwaukee." I decided not to mention Aric. I didn't think it mattered at this point, but if there was a way to protect him I had to try.

"No one knows me as Tara in Zilwaukee," Tara said grimly.

"No, but someone recognized your picture. She said your name was Lola."

"What picture?"

"The ones on my phone that I took at that first party."

"I didn't see you taking any pictures."

"I wasn't hiding it."

Tara frowned. "Who recognized me?"

Uh-oh. "A waitress at a diner." Not a lie.

Tara seemed to think about it for a second and then her jaw set in a grim line. "It was Fern, wasn't it?"

"Who's Fern?"

"She never could mind her own business."

"Well, to be fair, I took the picture to her. She didn't seek me out."

"That's true," Tara said eyeing me. "This really is all your fault."

"Have you been talking to my mom?"

Tara smiled despite herself. "It's too bad. I was hoping I wouldn't have to kill you. You've put me in a very untenable position."

"Forget that for a second, how do you still look like you're twenty-two?"

Tara regarded me with a hint of mirth. She must have decided that it didn't really matter what she told me since she was going to kill me anyways. "It's a glamour."

"What's a glamour?"

"It's a spell," Paris had finally found her voice.

"You're a witch?" I was surprised. "I thought you were a wolf?"

"I'm both."

I turned incredulously to Paris. "You didn't tell me that was even possible."

"Why wouldn't it be possible?"

"I don't know – it's like double-dipping."

"She's not a potato chip," Paris grumbled.

Tara watched us argue with bemusement. "I can't believe you're my arch nemesis," she sighed.

"Your arch nemesis? You need to stop watching soap operas – or reading comic books – or whatever it is that you're doing."

Tara's previous amusement fled her face. "Do you really think making fun of me is the best way to go here?"

"Well, you're going to kill us anyway and I'm not big on groveling, so I don't see the point of that. Even now."

"The warrior to the end," Tara smirked.

"I'm not a warrior," I argued. "I'm just a person."

"You really have no idea what you are, do you?" Tara seemed to want an honest answer.

"You're like the fifth person to say that to me in the last few weeks," I admitted. "I don't have a clue what you're talking about."

Tara met my gaze solidly. "That's too bad."

"You could tell me."

"Even I don't know all that you are," she admitted. "And I don't think it's my place to tell you."

"Well, since I'm going to die and you're the only one that knows," I tried again.

"I don't have enough time," she said. "I might actually tell you if I had time."

"Why? What's going to happen now?"

Tara stood expectantly and turned to the other wolves. While we had been talking, they had constructed a crude bonfire. I noticed – with a certain amount of trepidation – that they had erected two crosses in the center of the bonfire. That couldn't be good.

Tara saw where my eyes had traveled and laughed out loud. For a second, I pictured her in a straight-jacket. I think sanity had fled Tara a long time ago – maybe when she was still known as Lola.

"Those aren't for you," Tara soothed.

"Well that's good." I forced a smile.

"Who are they for?" Paris' question was so quiet I barely heard it.

"Those are for our special guests," Tara smiled evilly. "What I have planned for the two of you is much, much worse."

Well, that was comforting.

I didn't get a chance to ask who the "special guests" were. I heard a commotion from inside the house and I saw two figures being wrestled out to the backyard. One was clearly a male and the other was clearly a female.

I strained to see if I could recognize them – but they both had canvas sacks over their heads.

The wolves forced them to the crosses and proceeded to tie them up like they were creepy scarecrows. Scarecrows that were still alive and struggling desperately for their lives.

"They're stringing them up like Jesus Christ," Paris breathed.

Huh. I hadn't noticed that symbolism.

"They're not crucifying them," I offered. At least I hoped that wasn't the next step. From what I could tell, their arms were just being spread eagle and tied to the cross arms. Their feet were drawn together and tied around the bottom of the crosses – a mere two inches above the bonfire area.

"Well, that's a small favor," Paris tried for a lame joke. She looked pained when she finished.

I put my hand reassuringly on her arm. "We'll figure something out," I promised.

"You don't mean that," Paris said.

"I mean it. I just don't know if it's feasible," I admitted.

We both turned our attention to the crosses – where Tara walked up and dramatically removed the bags from her guests' heads.

I don't know what I was expecting – but seeing Rafael's disheveled black locks tumble down around his shoulders wasn't it.

When I turned to see who was trussed up beside him I practically choked. It was Brittany.

37 THIRTY-SEVEN

My heart felt like it was going to leap out of my chest. That's when it wasn't lodged in my throat. This couldn't be happening.

I glanced at Paris – but her eyes were glued on the scene in front of us. I think she'd lost the ability to blink, let alone speak.

Rafael's eyes searched the crowd and landed on me. He seemed surprised to see me. Frankly, I didn't blame him.

Brittany just seemed confused. "What is going on?" She sounded like a wounded bird.

Rafael slid his gaze sideways and took in Brittany's disheveled appearance. He immediately turned his attention back to me. Tara noticed and she shifted her gaze back and forth between us.

"Just how well do you two know each other?"

"I already told you," I snapped. I glared at her as I got to my feet. A steady growl went through the assembled wolves. I noticed they'd made a circle around us. I didn't like this one bit.

I scanned the crowd hopelessly. I didn't see any wolves that I recognized unfortunately – except for Brett. Why didn't that surprise me? Brett sidled through the assembled wolves and took his position next to Tara. They smiled at each other – and I couldn't help but notice the adoration washing over his face.

"Good grief," I lamented. "Are you two a couple?"

Tara frowned at me. "I told you I had a boyfriend."

"You didn't tell me he was a sociopath that drugged women."

I couldn't help but feel a little smug when I saw the confused look wash over her face.

"What is she talking about?" Tara turned to Brett with her hands on her hips. "You told me she made that up."

"She did," Brett averted his gaze.

"He's lying. That's a tell," I crowed.

Tara seemed to agree. "Were you drugging women to have sex with them?"

"I said no," Brett practically bellowed.

"I think she's right and you're lying."

Good. I'd sufficiently derailed the current stake burning for a few minutes. I needed to think.

Paris was looking to me for cues. Brittany was desperately struggling against her restraints – all the while making this really annoying mewling noise. And Rafael was just hanging there like he didn't have a care in the world. Well, actually, he kept shaking his head occasionally, but I got the impression he was more upset about his hair being out of place than anything else.

"You know what? You say that you're different, but you're a typical man," Tara was still raging. "It's all about you and your needs."

"Who found a body to substitute out for you to fake your death?" Brett wasn't backing down.

"Oh, big deal, you broke into the morgue. You're such a big man."

"What is your deal? Is it that time of the month?"

All the wolves sucked in a breath and looked at Tara to see what her reaction would be.

"Oh, that's always your excuse for why I don't want to sleep with you," Tara complained. "Did you ever think it's you?"

"Me? I am great in bed."

"Who told you that?"

"Anyone I've ever slept with."

"Well, they're lying."

"Excuse me?"

"Just a tip, jackrabbit humping me isn't going to get me off. It's not going to get anyone off but you."

"You screamed like it got you off."

"Yeah, you imagined that. I have never screamed during sex with you." Tara focused her eyes back on me. "What is it with all guys thinking they're awesome at sex?"

I'd often wondered that myself. "I think they learn it from porn."

Tara thought about it a second. "That makes sense. Porn isn't even remotely realistic and yet men act like the second they climb on you that you're having an orgasm. They're so stupid."

Brett looked irate. The rest of the wolves just looked confused. I could only hope they were as stupid as they looked.

"Can you do anything?" I hissed to Paris.

"Like what?"

"I don't know, can you start them on fire?"

"I'm not that kind of witch."

"What kind of witch are you?"

"I'm a solitary practitioner."

"I don't know what that means."

"It basically means I can read people's auras and make a few potions."

"You can read people's auras? Well that should be helpful."

"No one needs your sarcasm."

Tara was still belittling Brett. If I had to guess, his package had shrunk to the size of a carrot stick and raisins. On second thought, it probably looked like that all the time. That would explain why he was always overcompensating.

I looked up and met Rafael's steady gaze again. I guess I was hoping he'd figure his own way out of this mess, because I was certainly at a loss for ideas.

Tara and Brett had finally stopped sniping at each other. Crap.

"We are gathered here tonight to make our offering to Samhain," Tara started in an ominous voice. Good grief.

"Halloween isn't for another week," I offered. What? I was trying to help.

"I know," Tara acknowledged with a shrug. "We're all busy on Halloween. No one wanted to give up the big Halloween party."

Oh.

"So, what are you trying to accomplish here?" I knew I was getting desperate to stall for time, but I didn't know what else to do.

"We're sacrificing two tributes to appease Samhain," Brett answered simply.

"Why?"

"So he will reward us."

"With what?"

Brett looked blank. He turned to Tara. "What are we asking for again?"

"We're not asking for anything," Tara sighed. "We're just trying to appease our God."

Something occurred to me. "You're lying."

Tara turned a glare in my direction. "I am not."

"You don't even believe in this Samhain nonsense. You're just doing this as a cover to kill Rafael." I don't know why I said it. The minute I uttered it out loud, though, I knew it was the truth.

Tara looked uncomfortable. I knew I'd hit the nail on the head.

Brett turned to her expectantly. "That's not true. Is it?"

"When you saw Rafael at the bar that night you freaked out." I still had no idea why. "You faked your death. You did that really quickly, by the way. Kudos. Then, when you found out that I knew Rafael, that's when you really freaked out."

Brett didn't look convinced. "We've had this planned for weeks."

"Yeah, since Rafael saw Tara."

Brett turned to Tara with a questioning look. He didn't say anything, but I could see his mind working. It looked like it was taxing him.

I turned to Rafael. "What's the deal between the two of you?"

Rafael seemed surprised to be addressed. "I've known her. For a long time."

"Since she was Lola, right?"

Rafael looked surprised. "You've been busy, Nancy Drew."

"And how did you know Lola?"

Rafael set his jaw. "Lola has been killing my kind for 20 years. She started with my father."

"You had a father who was a vampire? I thought you had to get bit to be a vampire?"

"Not always."

My head was spinning. Maybe I should have paid more attention to Blake and his teachings. I was starting to feel guilty for just dismissing him. *Cripes. Who needs that?*

"You're father had it coming," Tara seethed. "He hunted my family for years."

"Maybe that's because you were evil," Rafael countered.

I could believe that.

"We were not evil! We were just trying to survive."

Rafael glowered at Tara. I had no idea which version of truth was the right one. I just knew that I wasn't in the mood to watch a human barbecue.

"Why don't you just agree to disagree?" I offered.

"It's too late for that."

I figured that's what she would say.

I turned to the assembled wolves. "So, you're willing to kill two people for a grudge match between a witch and vampire?"

Brett shrugged. "We don't really have a choice now do we? And, by my count, we're going to have to kill four people."

"He's talking about us," Paris muttered.

"Thanks, I figured that out." She really was no help in a crisis.

"How are you going to explain the disappearances of all four of us?"

"Vampires disappear all the time," Tara explained.

"And three roommates?"

Tara paused.

"She has a point," Brett looked worried.

"We'll go back to the dorm after this and take all their stuff. People will think they all took off together."

"Why would we do that?"

"Who knows? The police won't look that hard. Trust me. I put a very simple glamour on a week-old body and they not only believed it was me, but never questioned the disappearance of the other body. Cops are stupid."

After meeting the two idiots that came to our room, I couldn't help but agree. *Double crap.*

"Light the fire," Tara instructed Brett.

He reached into his pocket, pulled out a lighter and obediently made his way over to the stacked wood.

"What about your little ceremony?" I asked desperately.

"You've erased the need for that," Tara said with a wicked smile. "Thank you. All that pretense was going to be tiresome."

That's me, always being helpful.

I got to my feet again. I had no idea what I was going to do. I just knew I couldn't let this happen.

Brittany picked this moment to start wailing. "What did I ever do to you?"

Tara regarded her like a bug on a windshield. "You just happened to be in the wrong place at the wrong time."

"I won't tell anyone. I promise. Just let me go."

"I don't believe you. You have a moral code. A really, really annoying moral code that no one – not even you – can live up to."

"I thought we were friends," Brittany whimpered.

"You thought wrong," Tara said simply.

"Why did you come here?" I asked.

"I decided it would be fun to go to college," Tara said. "You saw where I grew up. I never had a chance. Now that I had the money, I didn't see why I couldn't give it a shot. It wasn't exactly what I thought it would be – and that was before Rafael showed up and ruined everything."

"What did you think it would be?"

"I don't know. Parties. Fun. Not all these classes and annoying little boys and girls in heat."

"We're teenagers. Of course we're in heat. That's what teenagers do."

"I may still look like a teenager, but I haven't been one in a very long time. I guess I forgot." She was so matter-of-fact. It was grating.

"Why not just leave?"

"Oh, I will. After I tie up a few loose ends."

Brittany was now sniveling like a two-year-old that had her favorite toy taken away. I wanted to smack her myself. Of course, I wasn't the one tied to a pyre.

"And what loose ends would those be?"

I had no idea where the voice came from – but I recognized it. Aric had arrived. Great. He was big, but he wasn't big enough to take out thirty wolves and a crazy woman. We were all going to die together.

I searched the crowd for him. I noticed the circle of wolves opening to the left. I was surprised to see that Aric wasn't alone. He had a cadre of wolves with him – including Will.

Aric's gaze met mine. "You can't keep out of trouble, can you?"

"How did you find us?"

"I followed your scent."

"That's a little gross."

Will was looking at the both of us. He didn't look happy. At least he was here, though.

Tara stepped to the middle of the circle and frowned when she saw Aric and the other wolves. "What do you think you're doing?"

"I'm not letting you do this."

"Why do you even care? It's just a vampire and three little girls."

"I don't care about the vampire," Aric said, sliding a disapproving glance to Rafael. "I care about the little girls."

I think I'd just been insulted.

For the first time that night, Tara looked nervous. I took that as a good sign. I saw that the rest of the wolves that she had amassed also looked uncomfortable. Brett stepped forward. I could tell he was jittery.

"I command you all to go back to the frat house."

Aric snickered. "Sit down."

I was a little impressed at Aric's swagger. I was even more impressed when Brett obeyed him.

"What are you doing?" Tara was incredulous.

Brett averted her gaze.

I couldn't help but notice that some of Brett's wolves had started slinking away into the dark. Tara noticed, too.

"Where are you wimps going?"

"That's the way to appeal to them," I smirked. "Call them names."

Tara pointed her finger at me angrily. "Shut your mouth."

"You shut your mouth."

"No, you shut your mouth."

"Will you both shut your mouths?" Rafael was looking irritated. He met Aric's gaze. "You want to get me down from here?"

"Not particularly," he growled. Aric turned to me. "Go cut him down."

I skirted around Tara and made my way to Rafael. I wasn't keen on being bossed around. I figured having Rafael free could only be helpful at this point, though. I plucked the knife from Brett's hands. He didn't argue.

"Don't you untie him," Tara warned.

I didn't listen to her. I quickly cut Rafael's bonds and then moved over to Brittany. Rafael rubbed his wrists, but he didn't move from the middle of the woodpile. After I freed Brittany, she stumbled over to Paris and dissolved into tears as she wedged herself next to her on the picnic table bench. Paris absently rubbed her back. Her eyes never left Tara, though. She was still dangerous.

When I turned back to the scene, I noticed that there were only about five wolves from Tara's contingent left. Aric's wolves could easily take them. Tara was the wild card – and it didn't look like she was backing down.

"That's it," she bellowed. "I will handle this myself you cowards."

Tara reached into the inside pocket of her jacket and pulled out … a gun. *What the hell?*

"A gun? You brought a gun to a werewolf fight? That is unbelievable."

"What did you think I was pulling out? A magic wand?"

"Actually, yes."

"You're so naïve."

"Let me guess. There's silver bullets in there?"

"But of course."

"I was joking."

"I'm not."

I noticed Aric had shifted slightly when she pulled the gun. To his credit, though, he didn't back away.

"Can those kill you?" I was looking at him.

Aric nodded absentmindedly. He never took his eyes from the gun.

"You can't shoot him," I appealed to Tara.

"Why? Because you love him?"

"I don't love him," I scoffed. "I just met him. This isn't some *Twilight* bullshit."

"Those books are total crap," Tara agreed.

"I love those books," Brittany sniffed.

"You would," Tara snorted.

Tara pulled back the hammer on the gun and leveled it at Aric. "You ruined this for me."

"You ruined it for yourself."

"Oh, good grief." Rafael had moved from his spot on top of the bonfire. He picked up a branch from the bonfire and shoved it through Tara's chest from behind. I saw what he was doing as he was doing it and somehow my mind was having trouble registering what was happening.

Tara didn't look like it hurt. In fact, she looked more surprised than anything else. She cast a glance over her shoulder and met Rafael's gaze. "Congratulations," she rasped. "You killed my entire clan."

"Right back at you," Rafael seethed. He then wrenched the branch back out of Tara and she crumpled. To be more exact, her clothes crumpled. She was gone.

Paris and Brittany gasped. I curiously moved over to the pile of clothes and nudged them with my foot. There was nothing there, though.

"Where did she go?"

"She's dead."

"There's no body."

Rafael shrugged. "She's dead. Don't worry."

"Chatty as always, I see."

"What do you want me to say?"

"How about thank you? You know, for saving your life?"

"You didn't save my life."

"The hell I didn't."

"Is this really the time for this?" Paris was trying to disengage herself from Brittany's clingy embrace. It wasn't exactly working.

"How do you figure you saved him?" Aric was looking nonplussed.

"Because if I hadn't been here they would have started him on fire long before you showed up."

"You don't know that."

"Oh, please. I suppose you want credit for saving us."

"Well, I did."

"Did you ever consider this might not have happened if you just told me what you knew instead of hiding like a little ferret for the past couple of weeks?"

"What are you talking about?"

"You knew that Tara was Lola after we went to Zilwaukee."

"Why would you go to Zilwaukee with him?" Will had finally found his voice.

"Why do you care?"

"I'm just curious," Will started studying his shoes.

"We went to try and track down Tara's family. When we got back, he disappeared like ... like a disappearing guy."

"Nice analogy."

"Screw you."

"You people are unbelievable!" Brittany was on her feet and she wasn't exactly what I would call happy. "I almost died tonight and all you care about is your little soap opera."

"Simmer down," Aric ordered.

Brittany was having none of it. "You are not the boss of me!"

"Brittany, calm down."

Brittany swung around and grabbed the arm of my coat. "And you! You have been keeping secrets. Secrets that could have gotten me killed."

"Well, if you had listened to me and stayed away from my ex-boyfriend none of this would have happened to you."

Brittany looked chastised.

"Why do you care if she hits on your ex-boyfriend?" Aric was glaring at me.

"That's a good question." Great. Now Rafael was getting involved in the situation.

"Why do you care?" Aric was now facing Rafael.

"Why do you care?"

You know who didn't care anymore? Me. I was suddenly tired. I turned and started to walk away from the house. The wolves that had come with Aric parted to let me through. None of them said anything. I couldn't help but think they were relieved to see me go.

"Where are you going?"

"To take a shower and go to bed. You people make me tired."

EPILOGUE

T he rest of the term went by in a blur.

Brittany was back to her annoying self within a few days. It was almost as if she had forgotten what had happened. Unfortunately, whenever we got into an argument, she brought up the fact that my secrecy had put her life in danger. It was a long couple of weeks.

Paris and Mark were still flirting – but the relationship hadn't moved any further. Mark was recruiting her for the monster academy. She hadn't committed yet, but I had a feeling she would eventually. I didn't know how to feel about that.

I'd run into Will on campus about a week after the event. Things had been cordial, but unfamiliar.

I hadn't seen Rafael. I was actually relieved about that. I didn't know what to say to him. I was torn between thanking him and smacking him. He had shoved a piece of wood into the chest of my roommate, after all. Sure, she was going to burn him at the stake, but the whole thing was still so surreal.

Aric had stopped by the dorm. I'd made Paris lie and tell him I wasn't there. I wasn't ready to deal with him either.

Before we knew it, the semester was over and we were all going home for Christmas break.

"Things will be better next semester," Brittany announced brightly.

Yeah, she's not the quickest redneck at the frog pond.

I was actually relieved to find myself back in my old bedroom, surrounded by my childhood stuffed animals, and the familiar smells of home. Sure, it was a bummer to have my parents constantly watching my every move, but it was only two weeks, though.

As I went about my daily activities, I occasionally found my parents watching me thoughtfully. They could tell something was different, they just didn't know what. I had no intention of filling them in – at least not yet.

The day after Christmas, I was sitting on the couch and reading a magazine – someone needs to start the entire Kardashian clan on fire -- when there was a knock on the door.

It was winter in Northern Lower Michigan, so the days were getting shorter. It wasn't even 6 p.m. yet and already dark. When I opened the door, I got the surprise of my life.

"What are you doing here?" I looked over my shoulder. Neither of my parents was in the general vicinity.

"We need to talk." My guest pushed his way into the house without waiting to let me invite him in.

"We can talk when we get back to campus."

"This can't wait." My guest's dark hair was messy from the wind outside and his dark eyes were fierce.

"Now what? Another witch? Another stake burning?"

"No. The pack is coming for you."

Made in the USA
San Bernardino, CA
25 August 2018